CORRUPT PRINCE

IVY MASON

Photography by
PAPERBACK MODEL

We wear the mask that grins and lies,
    It hides our cheeks and shades our eyes,—
    This debt we pay to human guile;
    With torn and bleeding hearts we smile...

We smile, but, O great Christ, our cries
    To thee from tortured souls arise.
    We sing, but oh the clay is vile
    Beneath our feet, and long the mile;
    But let the world dream otherwise,
        We wear the mask!

EXCERPT FROM **WE WEAR THE MASK BY**
PAUL LAURENCE DUNBAR

ONE

Coulter

A DIAMOND IS ONLY A LUMP OF COAL UNTIL, GIVEN enough pressure, it becomes something people would pay thousands, if not millions, of dollars for.

My whole life, I'd been protected.

I was intimately aware of both my father's indifference and his brutality, but most of the time, my brother, Bourbon, took the brunt of it.

He also made sure that my work in the mafia was focused on the business end of things.

I'd seen plenty of tortured but only witnessed a few people killed. When *I'd* killed, it had only been in self-defense.

And, I'd been in love.

It was the kind that stole my breath away, the kind that lived with grandeur in my heart, making the clouds float about my head and the world swell with music.

It had been bigger than life itself, and I was so alive with it that nothing else existed in my life, except for her.

And even after she died, stopped breathing in my arms, I was protected still from the truth.

Naive. Useless.

I was as worthless as a lump of coal.

As I sat on the plane, watching my brother comfort the woman who reminded me of the woman I'd once loved, my chest burned with anger. Even in their anger and grief, you could feel the devotion and tenderness pulsing between them. They genuinely loved each other.

I tapped my fingers on my thigh, wrenching my eyes away from them, and instead stared out the window into an endless blue sky. There were no clouds, only a nothingness beyond, much like how I was feeling inside.

As soon as Bourbon revealed the family secret, that my pieceofshit father had been raping the love of my life in my home, only suites down from my own room, I'd taken it out on anything inanimate within reach.

I'd punched, kicked, screamed, letting out all the rage. The wrath of my fury was born and now, it was building inside me like a trapped animal. Focusing on my anger would give me strength to pull out my gun the moment I saw my father and blow his brains out.

I knew killing him would change something inside me, tear any innocence remaining and turn me into one of them.

Like a useless piece of coal, this world was going to burn me up, turning me into the ashes of what was once a human being.

But my humanity didn't matter any more. All that mattered was my revenge.

Torian finally landed the plane we'd confiscated from Dimitri's old crew, the man Rose had killed, her own revenge enacted, and I waited impatiently as it made its way down the runway. Once it turned into our private hanger, I immediately stood up and glared out the window. I was anxious to see my father's face before I killed him.

He was waiting for us on the tarmac, with a cold and stiff

stance. He had a new woman by his side, someone who wasn't my mother.

Because he'd gotten her killed too.

The new woman was young and pretty and probably a whore too.

I just hoped I didn't get too much blood on her pretty, pink dress.

As soon as the stairs lowered, I rushed down them, my hand going to my back, where my gun was tucked.

Before I even stepped onto the runway, I was shoved to the ground, a heavy weight on top of me and my arms pinned behind my back.

"Mr. King has requested no weapons be allowed when you greet him," a low growl from Benny, one of his loyal guards, sounded behind me. I grunted as a knee dug into my back and my face smashed into the hot concrete by a hand on my head.

"Please, Coulter. Don't hurt him. He has my sister."

I lifted my eyes to stare into Rose's gorgeous face. Her troubled green eyes filled with concern.

"Get off him."

The weight on me disappeared and then Bourbon was by my side. Grabbing my arm, he yanked upward, pulling me to my feet.

I grappled to stand without his assistance, noting that Benny had taken my gun. Once I was steady on my feet, I shoved Bourbon away. "I don't need your help."

I hated him right now.

He'd known all along that our father was raping Lily, and yet he did nothing.

He held his hands up in the air in surrender, trying to make light of the situation. "No problem, man."

I fixed my suit, straightening my shirt and tie before turning my back on them.

I couldn't look at them.

I turned to glare at my father, who was watching us with a slight curling upwards of his lips, his only emotion at seeing his prodigal sons return home. His stark blue eyes, the same color as Bourbons, were blank, apathetic.

But me, I burned with emotion.

Hatred.

Rage.

I didn't wish him dead; I wished him obliterated into nothingness. Not even a burial or his body burned to ashes to be thrown into the desert.

I wanted him to not exist.

He flinched at the look I gave him, which made satisfaction fill me.

Even though I had no gun, only a small pocket knife, I could still take the chance and race at him. I didn't need a weapon to kill this man, my hatred would be enough. I wanted to wrap my hands around his neck and watch the life slowly drain from his eyes.

It wouldn't be the first time I'd killed a man. Thanks to him, I had practice out in the desert.

It would be fitting justice to use the skills he'd forced me to learn to take him down.

And yet, I couldn't make myself do it. If I killed my father, they would kill Rose's sister.

Even though I hated my father with every cell in my body, I loved Rose more, and I would grant her, her wish.

Not killing my father would be my gift to Rose, the woman who'd saved my brother.

Nodding my head, I shut down every emotion inside in order to gain control over myself. I would be cold and heartless, just like my father, because if I didn't, I would suffocate from the smothering weight on my chest.

"Fine." I turned away from his satisfied smirk, walking towards the back of the grey cargo plane where they were already unloading the crates of weapons and ozone. Bourbon had negotiated our safe return in exchange for it.

I wordlessly watched as they worked, pretending I wasn't paying attention but I was actually listening to every word between the three of them.

"I want to see my sister. You better not have hurt her or I'll--"

"Or you'll what? Kill me?" My father chuckled darkly. "I'd like to see you try. If Bourbon here couldn't do it before, what makes you think you could?"

His words shocked me. I never knew that Bourbon had tried to kill my father.

There was only one time when my brother's whereabouts had been unaccounted for, for days on end. When I was sixteen, he'd been gone for two months. When he'd returned, any light that had been in his eyes was completely gone. They were dead, just like my father's. He also moved more slowly, like mere movement was difficult for him.

The blood drained from my face when I realized that it was around the same time Lily had come to me that first night crying.

Had Bourbon tried to kill my father after he found out what had happened?

If so, I could imagine my father would've beat him to within an inch of his life. That would explain the time needed to recover, and the deadness in his eyes.

It could also be the reason Lily never told me the truth.

Once again, I realized how I'd been protected my whole life without knowing it.

Fuck! This was going to stop. Now.

"Maybe I'm smarter than Bourbon." She stared him down with a haughty look.

My father's hand clamped down on her arm and he drug her to him, his face red and mottled with rage. "If you know what's good for you, girl, you'll keep your mouth shut, or your sister will suffer."

I swiveled on my feet, anger surging through me, but Bourbon's hand snapped forward, instantly jerking my father's hand off of Rose. He stepped in between Rose and my father, his face calm and cool. Ice cold. The dangerous side of Bourbon had come out.

He was an inch taller than my father, and he stared down at him. "Touch her again and I will kill you."

"Bourbon," Rose's sweet voice interjected.

Bourbon shook his head. "No. You may have the upper hand here, Nero, but I will not tolerate you touching my fiancé."

"Fiancé?" My father's face went blank. "You mean you actually proposed to the girl?"

"Yes," I bit out, joining them, "he did. Do you have a problem with that?"

Instead of being angry like I thought he would be, my father grinned. "Of course not, why would I?" He stepped back, conceding to Bourbon. "In fact, it was my plan for the two of you to marry, even if you didn't want to. Word can't go around that my son went chasing after some tail, can it?" His cold gaze moved to Rose. "Of course not. We will announce to everyone that you are the lost Petrov princess, and that I've arranged the two of you to marry as an alliance between the Bratvas and the Kings. Nicholi has accepted it, and so will you. Is that clear?"

Rose was furious. I could see it in her clenched fists, her fiery gaze. "I want to see my sister. Make sure you haven't killed her already."

"Doctor?" My father tilted his head to the side, and the woman in the pink dress stepped forward, pulling something from her large black bag as my father continued, "I need some of Bourbon's blood. If he gives it to me without--"

"What do you need my blood for?" Bourbon snarled.

"If he gives it to me without a fight, I will let you talk to your sister on the phone." His gaze turned back to Bourbon. "If you don't, I will take it anyways, and order the sister to be killed."

Bourbon's hands clenched into fists and he stepped into my father's space, with spitting rage on his face. The calm and collected Bourbon was gone, replaced by someone who was quickly going to lose his control.

In that moment, I knew what my purpose was from here on out.

My father would always hang Rose's sister's life over her head like a guillotine. And, because of this, he would be able to control Bourbon.

It was my turn to be the protector. Bourbon and Rose deserved their happy ending.

I placed my hand on his arm, determined to defuse the situation or someone we didn't want harmed would end up dead. "It's just a little blood."

"Please, Bourbon," Rose said.

When Bourbon didn't tear his eyes away from my father, I continued. "He can't hurt you or Rose with it." I drew his attention away from our father, growling out. "I swear I won't let him."

"Fine," he snarled. Taking off his Armani suit jacket, he began to roll up his sleeve.

Smirking, my father gestured with his fingers and the doctor pulled the rest of her supplies out of the bag.

"You and Bourbon will be staying at a house in Summerlin," my father's sneer turned sharper, "away from the strip and our house."

"But—" Rose tried to interject but my father cut her off.

"That's the deal. I don't trust you anywhere near my business, or where I'm keeping your sister."

"Fine," Rose grit out, "but I want to see her. Face to face."

"You will," my father gave her a cold smile, "if, and when, I see fit. If I see that you two are on your best behavior, acting the doting couple, as well as the *obedient* children I know you can be, you will be allowed to see her. But on my orders only."

Rose scowled, folding her arms across her chest. "I want to talk to her *now*."

"Of course, dear," my father took out his phone and swiped at it.

As the doctor took a couple vials of Bourbon's blood, my father handed over his phone to Rose.

"Aster?" Rose began to cry, apologizing over and over, turning away from us to whisper into the phone.

Hearing Rose break down made something inside me go stark cold.

I hated, *hated* what my father was doing to her. To her sister. To Bourbon. He would burn the whole world down to get what he wanted.

With every tear that fell down her face, I bricked another stone in the wall around my heart.

I knew that in order to protect them, I was going to have to be just like him.

Cold. Unfeeling. Hard.

As emotionless as a piece of coal.

I was done being the useless brother.

From here on out, I pledged to burn *his* world down in order to save the people I loved.

TWO

Coulter

As soon as the cars pulled up to take Bourbon and Rose away, I followed my father to his, determined to step into my new role as the protector. I had to know my enemy to defeat him.

First, I was going to gain his trust. Then, as soon as his back was turned, I was going to stab a knife in it.

I was silent the whole ride to the house, only shifting on the luxurious black leather of the seat, studying him. He had two deep scratches on his neck and one on his face.

He had a lithe and athletic build, with muscular arms and legs, but it had been a long time since my father had gotten his hands dirty.

I watched, emotionless, as the "doctor" got on her knees in front of my father, her light-brown highlighted hair cascaded down her back in tight curls. She pulled his dick out to give him a blow job.

Right in front of me.

If this was the kind of shit Bourbon had had to put up with his whole life, no wonder he'd become a robot.

My father just stared at me with a smirk on his face, hardly giving her any attention until, finally, he gave in to the moment. Grasping the back of her hair, he thrust forward, and she choked on his dick.

As he shoved her deeper into his crotch, his lips twisted even wider.

She was suffocating but he didn't care, and he didn't release her until he'd blown his load down her throat. She sucked in a breath, tears streaming down her face and her makeup smeared as she swallowed, then licked him clean.

Usually I didn't mind a girl getting dirty like that but watching someone do it to my father made disgust roll in my stomach.

When she was done, she got up and sat next to him, staring at the floor. He zipped up his pants and pulled out his phone, tapping on it and ignoring her. When we drove inside the gates to the house, he commanded his driver, Brett, to stop, then finally turned his attention to her. "Get out."

Her mouth dropped open. "But--"

"I need to talk to my son, and you have work to do." He nodded to her medical bag, where she'd stashed the vials of Bourbon's blood.

"You can at least drop me off at my car." Her voice was incredulous. The walk from the gate to the house wasn't a long walk but it was still a ways.

"Like I said," his voice was a cold sneer, "I need to talk to my son before we get to the door."

She stared at him for a moment, as if she was going to stand up to him. Her lips parted but, at the dark glare he gave her, they snapped shut. She crawled out of the car, grabbing her bag before slamming the door behind her.

As soon as the car began to move again, he turned his attention to me, not giving her a second thought. "Before I bring you into this house, I need to know if I can trust you."

I gave him a hard look. "I kept an eye on Bourbon, made sure he didn't do anything to disgrace the family name."

"Like running off after some snatch?"

"Like you said, she's not some whore, but Petrov royalty. Their union makes business sense."

"You don't care about business. If so, you wouldn't have killed Dimitri."

"Dimitri was a cunt. He was too emotional. If he hadn't been so worried about getting her back, we'd have made hundreds of thousands by now, and he'd still have his head attached to his neck."

My father scowled. "Why did he care about her so much anyway?"

I shrugged. "Does it matter? He's dead. Nicholi is making the decisions now." I leaned back, detaching myself from this conversation in order to convince my father that I was on his side. "The ozone we have won't last. The crates we've captured will keep them busy for a little while, but we need to make a new alliance with Nicholi. I'll do some research. Figure out what's important to him."

From what Knight had told me, Nicholi was just as sadistic as Dimitri, if not more.

"Once we have what he wants," I continued, "I'll set up a meeting between us. Bourbon was too accommodating. All we need is leverage, then it's easy to broker a deal."

My father studied me impassively as we pulled up to the door. "Fine," he finally answered, "we'll see if I can trust you. Prove it to me by taking care of the sister. She's in one of the guest bedrooms. You will be in charge of keeping her happy. Make sure she is fed and has the necessary supplies."

I gave him an astonished look, surprised that he even cared about all that.

"Don't be stupid. I'm well aware that this girl is my leverage over keeping Bourbon from slitting my throat."

"Fine," I agreed.

"I'll let Marisol know. But be aware. She's a difficult woman, so keep a watchful eye on her. If she goes missing, your head will roll. Is that clear?"

I nodded and he shifted forward, ready to step out of the car.

"There's one more thing. I have another prisoner in the room next to Aster's. If you really want to take a step up in the family, I'll need you to take care of him, too. Make sure he has just enough food to keep him alive, nothing else. He can have toilet paper and a bar of soap to keep him from stinking up the house, but that is all."

"Okay." The torture part was already beginning.

"Listen to him, be friendly with him if he wants to talk, then report everything back to me." He laid a hand on my shoulder, giving me a dark, threatening look. "I can trust you with him, correct? If not, then I'll find someone else to do the job."

I nodded. "Of course."

"Good," he nodded, then he began to climb out of the car. "Marisol will show you where their rooms are." Then he stepped out and walked into the house without a backwards glance.

I waited a full moment after the door closed behind him before I leaned back into the seat, thinking.

Something was different. My father had never kept any prisoners at the house.

It was too distasteful and dirty. He had back rooms in warehouses for that.

But now, he had two prisoners in the house, and had taken vials of Bourbon's blood.

There had to be a reason for all this, and I was going to find out why.

Brett lowered the partition. "Do you need to go somewhere, sir?"

"Take me back up the driveway. Let's bring my father's new whore to her car."

James frowned. "I don't think Nero would like that sir."

"I don't fucking care what he would like."

The edges of Brett's lips trickled upwards in a suppressed smile, and he nodded. "Yes, sir," he said as he pulled the car around the circular driveway. The woman was in high heels and her dress was so short, it was riding up her ass. She was walking strange, as if she'd never worn heels before.

When we offered to take her to her car, she didn't hesitate and climbed in, thanking me. We were silent for most of the way and, after a while, I had to ask her. "What will Nero do with the blood?"

Her eyes widened and she clutched the bag closer to her torso, as if I was going to jerk it from her. "I can't tell you that."

I nodded, understanding, then let my eyes fall to her dress. "Are you a real doctor?"

"Of course I am."

"And do you usually dress like that for work?"

She shifted uncomfortably, pulling down her dress. "Not usually, but Nero thought it might be more appropriate when I work with him, given my new...duties."

I bit down on my lower lip, considering her. The woman didn't seem to be too happy with her new job.

Nero was probably forcing her to do whatever it was with Bourbon's blood that he wanted. Giving him a blow was just something he considered his perks by employing her.

I sighed, staring out the window, deciding I wasn't going to stand by and let my father do whatever the hell he wanted with the people around him.

As we dropped the woman off at her car, I resolved then and there that I was going to try to get the doctor out from under his thumb. I said my thanks to Brett, then climbed out of the car, taking in a deep breath as I stared up at the mansion.

I suddenly realized that I hadn't missed the place.

In fact, being back home felt like chains were wrapped around me again. It was stifling and suffocating.

I hated it.

And now, I had to feed and take care of Rose's sister.

As I walked through the front door, I clamped down on my emotions, determined I wouldn't let them affect me.

Marisol, the cook who had been in our family as long as I could remember, was waiting for me when I entered, holding a plate of freshly baked cookies and a smile. "Coulter. Estás aquí. You're home."

Something inside me loosened and I leaned over, giving her a hug and kiss on the cheek. She was short, barely reaching my chest, with bronzed skin and large, brown eyes. When she reached over, hugging me back, her plump body enveloped mine with warmth.

She didn't mention Bourbon and I figured my father must have informed her that Bourbon wasn't going to be staying here. Either that or she'd lived here long enough to know not to ask questions.

"Here," after she let me go, she thrust the plate of cookies at me.

"Thanks." I tried to smile, realizing that she was only trying to make me feel better. I stuffed a couple into the pocket of my Armani suit, because no one ever said no to Marisol. She turned and replaced the cookies with another tray of food, passing it over to me. "This is for the young lady."

She acted as if Aster was here voluntarily, a special guest in our home, instead of taken against her will. I guessed even the servants had their own ways of coping. "After you serve her, I will give you the other tray," she nodded, picking up another platter, "Nero said that he wants you to feed the man from now on."

I noticed that there was significantly better quality food on the plate that had Aster's food. It looked like my father was holding up his end of the deal to treat Aster well in exchange for the weapons and drugs.

Marisol began to walk up the stairs and I followed behind her, noticing that her straight, dark-brown hair had grown to the top to her waist. She turned left, heading down the hallway in the opposite direction of my father's rooms.

"Do you know who the man is?" I asked Marisol.

She clicked her tongue. "You know as well as I do that I don't speak of Mr. King's business, ever. Unless I want to lose my job."

Or your life, I wanted to add, though I didn't. However, that might not be correct. If my father would ever show anyone leniency, it would be Marisol. Her cooking skills were the only way to my father's heart, and not the blood that ran through our veins.

She'd worked for him since before my mom brought me to live here and, from what I could gather, since Bourbon was a baby too. She'd probably been the only woman in his life for this long.

As we walked, I glanced around, looking for my younger brothers. I wasn't surprised that they weren't waiting for me when we arrived, but I'd hoped to at least talk to them. My mom had asked me to keep an eye out for them.

"Where are the twins?"

At this, she pressed her lips into a firm line, betraying her disapproval. "Mr. King shipped them off to a private school in Atlanta."

I nodded, understanding now why it was so quiet. After a few more steps, we came to stop outside of the door to one of the many guest rooms we had in our house.

"Now," she said with a mischievous grin, "prepare yourself. She's an unruly one."

I gave her a confused look but she didn't say anything more, just unlocked the door with a key that hung around her neck.

"What kind of mischievousness are you up to?" I asked her, not able to hold back my chuckle as I opened the door. She shook her head, only giving me a secretive amused look. It suddenly fell away when her eyes landed on something in the room, then they widened in shock.

I turned, then froze when I saw the women in the center of the room.

Before us was a pile of broken furniture, and the odor of nail polish remover filled my nose.

A girl stood over the pile of broken furniture, with wild red hair, flashing green eyes, and a feral expression on her face. She held her hand up, gripping what looked like a sock.

Flames licked the edges, trickling upwards towards her fingers.

Her eyes met mine, and her lips curled upwards in a smirk. "You must be the Prince Charming."

Then she dropped the sock, setting the furniture on fire.

THREE

Aster

THE MAN WHO BETRAYED ME HAD A CHARMING SMILE AND a picture of Rose.

It was the kind of smile that you immediately noticed, even from across the room. On first appearance, it was perfect. Bright and enchanting, like the kind of smile worn by a great king in a Disney fairy tale.

It was only on closer inspection that you noticed the cold undertones, the deceptive gentlemanliness of it.

The picture of Rose was also, admittedly, a tad bit out of focus. She wasn't looking at the camera, but out at something beyond the sight of the photographer. She'd also had a scraggly looking dog by her side.

It was the sad look on her face that did it in for me, even though all of my instincts screamed that I shouldn't trust the man with the arresting, charming smile. I said goodbye to a father that I loved dearly, got onto a plane, and didn't look back.

When I arrived, Rose wasn't waiting for me at the airport like the charming man said she'd be.

In my defense, he'd just received a phone call stating that she'd been delayed.

Once again, I believed what he'd said, even though the pounding in my heart told me to run away as soon as the stairs to the private jet hit the ground.

But I thought of that picture and the sad look and *the scrawny dog*. She needed me, I could feel it.

Plastering on a smile, I took the crook of the elbow that the charming man offered me. He whisked me away from the fancy jet and into a fancy car and we went shopping, purchasing clothes for my impromptu visit.

I trusted the charming man.

Naively so—because that's what I did.

I trusted people, even when I shouldn't.

It was an issue of mine. I was working on it. Whatever.

Anyhow. I spent three full days shopping, pushing off my annoyance that Rose was still delayed, and pretended I wasn't worried. I politely accepted all offers for dinners, shows on the strip, and zip lining.

Finally, on the third night of outings and a bajillion excuses, I put my foot down and demanded to see Rose.

Suddenly, the *charming* man became Mr. Not-so-charming.

It was then that I was shoved in this room, dragged by three guards. Kicking and screaming, my insides twisted and turned as my instincts screamed 'I told you so'. That I never should've trusted that awful man.

After a day of being kept trapped in the room, the man entered, and I'd immediately pounced.

I was proud of the way I'd scratched up his face and neck with a nail file before his guards dragged me off him. I'd expected retribution but he'd only growled at me to *behave*.

Behave.

Like some mutt from off the street.

Like I was here voluntarily.

I'd show him a ferocious dog, all right.

Yelling, I'd jumped at him again, catching everyone off guard. It took his guards only seconds to grab me, but then I turned my wrath on them too.

It was only when Mr. Not So Charming called Rose, letting me talk to her only briefly, that I'd forced down all my anger and looked into Mr. Not So Charming's eyes and promised him with all the indignation and rage that I could muster, that I would kill him if he dared hurt her.

A cold smile was my only response, then a demand to give him the code to unlock my phone so he could text my Papa from it, something he'd confiscated as soon as they'd shoved me into this room.

And now, two days later, I was still stuck in this place, as if waiting for a death sentence.

Mr. Not So Charming had promised that if I behaved well, I would see Rose, but I was beginning to think that was a lie too.

I wasn't waiting around any longer. If this house was anything like my own, there would be guards outside my room and scattered along the property. I needed to test their security.

Thinking furiously, I strode back and forth in the room, stopping to stare out the window. There was a large expanse of a green lawn and the edges sparkled blue, as if there was a pool nearby. Though not as beautiful as the view from my own room at home, the sight was alluring, and hid the darkness within these walls.

My eyes scanned the area, sweeping back and forth, trying to figure out the outer edges of the property. Something flickered in the distance and I froze, narrowing my gaze to focus on the colorful dots.

Was there a garden back there? The ache in my chest was suddenly there again, my constant companion.

I pressed my fist to my chest, trying to focus in on the colors, though darkness flickered in my vision, making the aching in my chest swell and surge. I squeezed my eyes shut and took a deep breath.

There isn't time for this. I have more important things to think about.

Opening my eyes, I braced myself on the edge of my window sill and leaned out. My heart raced at the sight of the bushes below. I was two stories up.

Suddenly making my decision, I swirled back towards my room, racing towards the side drawer by my bed and yanked it open. There were two pads of paper, an expensive looking pen, a halfway empty pack of cigarettes and a lighter.

I grinned. *Perfect.*

I threw them aside, then went back for the other night stand. After an hour of sweat and cursing, I had a pile of broken furniture and crumbled paper in the middle of the room. Blown up condoms flit around the room like balloons, just for the fun of it.

I raised a tube of lube, squirting it over the pile, then the nail polish and remover came next.

"Whew." I fanned my face, wrinkling my nose. The smell was strong. Next came the lighter, and I grinned as I stared at the flickering flame proudly.

This was going to be awesome.

It took me several tries to get the sock I'd found to catch fire, but the lighter was one of those cool propane ones and worked long enough to get it going. Just as I was about to toss it onto the heap before me, the door knob rattled and it swung backwards.

A man entered.

And when I say man, I mean a *man*.

Sexy hot, with scruff around his jawline that I wanted to run my fingers through, and a mop of golden brown hair.

He was wearing a dark Armani suit, with a bright pink tie. It was so unusual that I did a double take. The soft color of it reminded me of the roses that lined the garden path at home, and they brought out his tanned, golden skin. He was laughing and, when he finally turned to face me, I was arrested by the beautiful smile, the easiness to his stride, the way he carried himself with a grace I could only be jealous of.

His face was gorgeous and beautiful and sensual, all at the same time, with a firm jawline and golden eyes that matched his golden skin and hair.

The sight of him was stunning, and it made me forget for one brief second that I was locked up in this cell of a room, away from my Papa and a home that I longed for.

That I'd just been trying to escape the confines of this room.

That the flames of the sock were climbing upwards towards my fingers.

And then his eyes settled on mine and I realized with a twisting of my stomach that he looked exactly like Mr. Charming from earlier. That same beautiful smile. Same gorgeous face. All except the eyes.

I scowled, immediately angry, my lips pursing into a line. This must be the younger version of the man keeping me prisoner.

The prince to the king.

I immediately hated him.

"You must be the Prince Charming," I sneered, then threw him a haughty look as I let go of the sock, just in time as the flames had begun to lick my fingers.

It took him a second to register what I'd done but it was a

second too late. The flames caught quickly and the flash of panic in his eyes was *everything*.

Soon, the dresser was torching and, smiling, I skipped over to the window. Without hesitating, I jumped.

I fell quickly, my stomach lurching, and landed harshly in the bushes below my window. It didn't deter me though, as I'd jumped from much higher heights back home.

It took me seconds to scramble out of the bushes and to my feet.

The sight before me was a lie.

The empty green expanse of lawn, the unmanned driveway leading away from the house, the appearance of freedom.

I knew my Papa's security well enough to know the truth beneath the surface.

"Hey!"

I glanced upwards, and the arresting face of Prince Charming peered out over the window.

Poop. I had to get going.

I leaped like a gazelle, jumping forward, quickly picking up speed. Arms pumping, my legs moved as fast as possible as I ran.

I headed to the front of the house and towards the driveway leading out of here. As soon as I skirted around the corner, I halted to a stop.

There were three guards with guns, spaced out. They were protecting the front door.

They didn't notice me so I turned, making a wide loop towards the side of the house.

My lungs began to burn, the harsh air scorching my airways.

Crapola, the air here was dry. I wasn't used to it.

Ignoring it, I picked up my pace. The wind whipped at my face and the dots of color I'd seen earlier grew bigger.

The dots transformed into flowers. It was a garden!

"You have to be gentle with the seedlings and patient with the perennials." The memory of my mama and me came to mind.

I suddenly felt alive. The sun was shining and the blue from the pool sparkled brighter. It was a beautiful day. The perfect kind to kick off your shoes and feel the grass squish between your toes.

I ran until I could barely breathe in the dry heat, even as my lungs and legs burned.

Until I could see the sparkle of the pool in my periphery.

Until I could see the garden, just ahead...

Suddenly, the horizon dotted with a wall of black. A line of men ran towards me from beyond the garden.

I could now see the large, stone fence, too tall for me to climb over.

I stopped suddenly, leaning over and heaving great breaths, trying to suck in air. It gave me a moment to think. Even if I could climb the fence, there was probably something else there to stop me. Probably more guards or an electric fence. I knew I wasn't getting out of here any time soon.

I straightened, pulling my spring dress with me. I stripped it off and threw it to the side, showing off my new lace bra and panties. The convergence of the guards ahead slowed, eyeing me warily. One of them shook his head.

I blew them a kiss, smirking.

They all stopped, shifting uneasily.

Good to know that they were the kind of men who had restraint.

I chuckled to myself, just as a firm body slammed into me from behind, shoving me to the ground.

FOUR

Coulter

It had been that goddamn smirk. The one she threw my way right before she'd dropped the flaming sock onto a pile of busted up furniture.

By the time I'd torn my eyes away from the *raging inferno in the middle of the guest room,* I caught the flash of her red hair before she'd sailed out the window.

The woman didn't even hesitate. She'd just jumped, falling two stories into the bushes below, then took off like it was *her tail* on fire.

I'd had no choice but to jump after her, trusting that Marisol would get the flames under control.

I gritted my teeth as I landed in the scratchy bushes, hating that I was reduced to chasing a she-devil across my lawn.

Surprisingly, she was quick as lightning and just as crazy. And when she stopped and stripped, showing off an athletic, tight body under that light orange dress, she was my nightmare come to life.

She might be a hellion in a cage but I was the one in chains.

Now, she was smooshed under me, halfway naked, and I had a hard on. Motherfucker, I hated my dick right now.

"Get off me!" she squealed, barely intelligible with her face in the grass.

"Promise you won't run anymore," I demanded.

"Fine! I won't run."

I hesitated, then sat back on the thick grass, pulling away from her to give her space.

She scrambled onto her feet, coming up swinging. Emerald eyes flashed as she socked me right in the cheekbone.

Yelping in surprise, I fell onto my back and heard the sound of my father's guards laughing.

Scowling, I rose to my feet, then took off, springing after her as she began to sprint away from me again.

It only took me a few steps to tackle her to the ground and, this time, I didn't hesitate to subdue her. Despite her squealed protests, I yanked her to her feet and threw her over my shoulder like a sack of flour.

She immediately grabbed my belt and yanked.

It was so unexpected, I lost my hold over her, and she slithered down my body, falling into the grass.

Growling in frustration now, I turned to see her scrambling to her feet. I pounced, landing on her. We tussled in the grass, my hard body over hers.

I was suddenly aware of her softness under me, skin like silk and perfectly sized breasts pressing up into my chest. Her white, lace bra and underwear reminded me of sweetness and innocence. But her red hair was wild and tangled, and freckles dusted her cheeks, flushing down her chest like a blush. Her beautiful emerald eyes flashed with anger and indignation. Her unbelievably strong arms and legs wrapped around my waist as she tried to push me onto my back.

I was immediately hard again as she pressed up against me,

imagining us doing something *very* different. Her hot and sweaty naked body withering under mine.

I grinned. *She would be a fucking pleasure to tame.*

Gripping her shoulders, I pressed her into the ground, hot anger shooting through me. I *wasn't* attracted to this feisty nightmare of a woman. In fact, I was determined to hate her, *and all women*, until the end of fucking time. They had no relevance in my life, *especially Rose's sister.*

"Be still, woman."

"Why should I?" She spat out, still struggling under me, which was only making my dick harder. I switched tactics and gripped her neck in a harsh hold, leaning down to stare into her eyes, my voice cold and uncaring.

"If you ever want to see your sister again, you will do what I say, exactly how I say it, and the second I command it."

"Chinga tu madre," she spit out at me, her eyes narrowing.

I knew enough Spanish to know that she'd just cussed at me. I squeezed harder and sexy, heart-shaped lips parted in a surprised exhale. Her body stilled, her hands going to my wrist. I was cutting off her breath but she continued to squirm.

"Rose is getting married in two weeks." Her eyes widened at the news and she suddenly stilled. I took advantage of it by tucking her hands between my thighs, continuing. "If you'd like to be there when she ties the knot with my brother, I suggest you learn some manners."

Her lips parted again, trying to take a breath, and I let go of my harsh hold on her neck. I wasn't trying to kill the little monster. She sucked in air, her words coming out in a rush. "If you assholes are forcing her to marry your brother, I will wait until you're sleeping, then I will slit your neck from ear to ear."

I burst out in laughter at the ridiculousness of the idea. First, she would never be able to get out of her room, I'd make sure of that. Second, the fact she thought she could not only get through the many guards from her room to mine, then manage to catch me unaware, was hilarious.

I'd slept with one eye open since I was thirteen and would hear her the instant she opened my door.

I'd have my gun trained on her in two seconds.

"What's so funny?" she scowled.

"You wouldn't even make it three steps into the room. And even if you could, which you wouldn't, I'd shoot you before you would even *think* about how to kill me."

"I just told you," she huffed a breath, blowing her hair out of her face, "I don't have to think about it. I plan on slitting you from one ear to the other."

I raised an eyebrow, feeling amused at the redheaded nightmare beneath me. "You wouldn't even nick my skin."

"You afraid, pretty boy?"

"You couldn't even get your hands on a knife."

"I don't need a knife to cut you." It was her turn to smirk. "Besides, you'd be surprised at how resourceful I can be."

I shook my head, chuckling. "Sure, little ginger." I reached forward, curling a strand of her red hair around my finger and tugged on it.

She scowled. "My name isn't Ginger."

"I don't care what your name is." Sitting up but still pressing my thighs together to keep her still, my hands went to my belt, unbuckling it. Her eyes widened as I slid it from my pants. "Your job from here on out is to be a good little girl and do what I say, m'kay?"

Suddenly her hand slid out from between my thighs, striking upwards towards my stomach. Dropping my belt, I grabbed her wrist, just in time to stop her from plunging a knife into my abs.

My knife. The one I'd been wearing only seconds earlier.

Growling and growing angry, I jerked the knife from her

hands and tossed it to the side. Then I grabbed both her wrists and held them over her head.

She struggled against me but I leaned down, pinning her tight with my hips. I growled in her ear. "If you don't hold still, I'm going to turn you around, yank down the pretty little underwear you have on, and spank your ass red."

She sucked in a shocked breath, stilling, but her voice was an angry growl. "You wouldn't dare."

"Try me." My voice was ice cold. I was deadly serious. "I would love the opportunity."

"You do and I'll slice your nuts off in your sleep."

I chuckled darkly and, holding her wrists with one hand, grabbed my belt. "You talk a big game," bringing her wrists to my chest, I wrapped my belt around them, "but let's see if you can actually back up those big, fancy words with action."

She heaved, watching as I finished securing her wrists with the leather belt. "Give me the chance and I'll show you just how real my words are."

I jumped to my feet, keeping a wary eye on her in case she tried to run as I fixed my suit. "How about I give you every opportunity in the world?"

She ticked an angry eyebrow upward. "And how would you do that?"

Reaching down, I grabbed my knife and tucked it back into its holder. "I'll put you in my room. If you can manage to kill me, then feel free to escape."

She huffed a breath. "Like you'd actually do that."

Leaning down, I grabbed her elbow and pulled her to her feet, making sure not to twist her arm in the process. "Try me." I began to lead her back towards the house, nodding at the guards who were still watching us curiously to let them know I had it handled. "Then again," I continued as we walked towards the house, "if you kill me, it's highly likely you'll never see your sister Rose again."

She hitched a breath. "Are you really going to let me see her?"

For the first time, she revealed a vulnerability, but I squashed down any empathy I had for her.

This was just a job for me.

A way to keep my father happy until we figured out how to get out of the bind we were under.

And I *definitely* wasn't going to feel sorry for her.

Regardless of the fact that she was only a pawn on our chess board, with no reason to be in the situation she was in, she was part of the game, whether she wanted to be or not.

Whether we even wanted her to be, or not.

"I don't know, princess, you're just going to have to trust me and see." Remembering Marisol's cookies that were in my pocket, I pulled out the crumbled remains, disappointed.

Her eyes immediately went to them, lighting up in interest. "Are those chocolate chip?"

"They *were*." I shoved the biggest piece into my mouth, just to annoy her. She eyed them hungrily and I sighed, offering her the rest. "Want one?"

The piece disappeared into her mouth within seconds. After a moment, she sighed dramatically. "God! These are to die for!"

She snatched the rest from my hands before I could even offer them to her, and I had to close my eyes and look away from her when her tongue flicked out, licking the chocolate from those full, sensual lips.

Fuuck. This was going to be hell.

FIVE

Aster

TRUE TO HIS WORD, COULTER MOVED ME AND ALL MY stuff from the old, now smoky, room to his. Excitement had flit through me at the thought that I may have a chance to use this opportunity to my advantage.

To my dismay, I'd been locked up in his room for four days now and not once had I even seen him. Not to shower, change clothes, or even sleep.

The prick. His only redeeming grace was that every morning since, I awoke with a plate of cookies by my bedside.

Still, he was clearly cheating, promising to give me an opportunity to kill him and then not showing up for the tête-à-tête.

Disappointing, seeing as how I'd been thoroughly prepared to *partirle su madre,* kick his ass, since the day he'd locked me up in here.

He'd removed all his guns from the room but he hadn't bothered to search for any other weapons, which was a severe underestimation of my skills.

Silly boys.

I was as familiar with guns as I was the back of my own hand. I preferred rifles but handguns would do in a pinch. However, I was also the innovative type and had several potential weapons all scattered about the room, ready for when his lazy *culo* actually came to his room.

While I was *awake*.

I mean, did he even really live here?

It didn't look like it.

The beer in his mini fridge was probably a hundred years old and he had very few personal items. There was only one framed photo, of him when he was a kid with another boy. Their arms were slung around each other, bright grins on their faces, even though their eyes were a bit wary, as if, even at a young age, they'd seen dark things.

The rest of the room had very little personality, with grey and black overtones, framed artwork that might show up in any hotel, and a large, comfy bed. The only interesting thing about it was the shelf of books that looked like it hadn't been touched in years.

It was also spotless.

Well, that was before I got here. *Ha.*

Now it was a mess.

I mean, don't get me wrong. I was, possibly, a bit spoiled by my Papa. I mean, maybe I was the apple of his eye, the jewel of his crown, the center of his heart. After my mama died, my Papa made sure I had everything I needed. I had no limit on my spending, and had private tutors in art, computer science, and the piano.

He also gave me the large garden in the middle of our courtyard, allowing me to take over my mama's old hobby and grow it into my own personal garden of Eden.

However, I was still responsible. Without mama, I took on

the responsibilities of taking care of my precious Papa, cooking and cleaning after him better than any old maid.

But. Kidnapping men didn't get the same treatment.

I grinned as I took in the sight of my new bedroom. Prince Charming's clothes were randomly thrown about, along with his fancy watches and ties. The pictures on the wall were now all upside down. My bra hung from the light fixtures and hair ties were on the knobs of his dresser. A pair of his boxer briefs were stretched across the top of a lamp.

I'd also casually tossed the boring-looking books off his shelves and placed those that looked interesting enough to read in a pile by his bed.

If he was going to keep me locked up in here, the least I could do was entertain myself.

And, admittedly, I was having a little bit of fun.

I laid back on Prince Charming's mattress, holding a book in my lap and lit one of the cigarettes from the pack I'd found in my old room.

I wasn't much of a smoker, but the smell reminded me of my Papa.

After breathing in the pungent smell of herbs, I crushed the tip on his nightstand and took a swig of the ridiculously expensive wine that I'd found hidden under his bed.

I'd had to smash the top of the bottle open, leaving the neck with the cork still inserted on the counter. So, the edges of the glass bottle were jagged and sharp, but that didn't deter me.

And Lord, the taste was to die for. The silky flavor slid down my throat. So rich. So sensual, it tasted like I was touching the very soul of my *bendito Dios*, Himself.

Or maybe I was a bit tipsy, I wasn't quite sure.

I took another sip, then squinted my eyes, trying to see how much I'd already drunk.

It looked about half-way full.

I frowned, disappointed. I was certain I'd had more, but, no matter, I'd fix that soon enough.

I stared down at the book delicately placed on my stomach, trying to read it, but the words were a little bit fuzzy.

The lock jingled and my eyes shot to the clock, hoping it was the cook who would talk to me sometimes. Unfortunately, it was too late for Marisol, unless she was bringing me a two a.m. snack.

Which would be perfect, actually. I did miss my chili and lemon peanuts.

The door slammed backward and my hope was squashed when Prince Charming himself appeared in the doorway.

He leaned against the doorjamb, blinking lazily as his eyes roamed the room. Pride filled me as his face grew darker and darker.

He didn't like what I'd done to his room.

And then his eyes landed on the bed, slowly moving from its rumpled state, up to my bare legs.

I was wearing one of his button-up shirts and a loose tie around my neck. I'd only bothered to button up the bottom ones, leaving a top notch view of my cleavage.

Sensuality was just as much of a weapon as a gun.

I smirked, opening my legs just a little bit. Enough to tease him. His eyes narrowed in on my panties but they didn't settle there. They climbed upwards, taking in his large shirt, the curves of my breasts...

Finally, they settled, not on my face, but on the wine in my hand.

He face darkened, turning into a storming rage as his back straightened. The lazy, exhausted look on his face was gone in an instant.

I burped.

His eyes moved, *finally*, to my face, and I gave him a snarky grin. "Hola."

"Where did you get that wine?" His jaw flexed.

Oh, he was really pissed. I took another gulp from the bottle, sighing loudly when I was done. "From under your bed, duh."

He suddenly strode forward, his long legs eating up the distance between us in mere seconds. His face was a raging storm, his eyes centered on the wine bottle in my hands.

Fear sparked in my chest, making my heart pound loudly in my ears.

For the first time since I'd been here, I was afraid for my life.

I threw the book off my lap, then jumped from the bed and skirted across the room.

"Aster," he growled, easily skating around the bed to chase me around the room. "Give me that bottle."

He surged at me so quickly that panic made me forget the fact that I could use the bottle as a weapon and instead, I swiveled on my feet, thrusting it at him.

"Here. You can have it. It's not that good, anyways."

He growled, grasping the bottle and holding it to his chest protectively.

Jeez, what was his deal? Protective much over some stupid alcohol? Maybe he was an alcoholic.

He marched over to the dressers and unceremoniously placed it on the top. "Ruined now." He seemed to be speaking more to himself than me. Placing both hands on the drawers, he stared at the empty space over them for what felt like forever, taking in a deep breath.

Laughter bubbled up inside me but I swallowed it down. He appeared angry and maybe, I was still slightly buzzed. Yes. Definitely still buzzed.

"Don't ever touch that again, is that clear? Or I will strip every single thing from this room and you will eat nothing but bread and water every day for the rest of your life."

He still wasn't facing me and a small, brief, semblance of guilt began to fill my chest.

"Are you okay?"

He turned, snarling at me. "I'm fucking peachy. Now get on the bed."

Any compassion for him shriveled up like a grape in the sun. "Why? I'm not tired."

He began to stalk towards me, his golden, stormy eyes on mine. I took two steps backwards, my throat suddenly dry as his angry steps drew closer.

It was suddenly there, that warm tingling feeling that started in my belly and spread in between my thighs.

Attraction.

His face was so beautiful, even in his anger, that it could be carved by Michelangelo. His furious gaze reminded me of an angry prince or god or something.

Temptation.

Sin.

Desire.

I swallowed down the knot in my throat, steeling myself.

I wouldn't have drunk his stupid, *special* wine if I hadn't been locked up in in his room.

I stood my ground, facing him down with my own wrath, my fingers going behind my back to the pen tucked in my underwear. As soon as he was close enough, I jumped.

He caught me, surprised, and I raised my arm to stab him with the sharp end of the pen.

Reacting quickly, he dropped me to raise his arm. The pen landed in his forearm.

He growled and shoved me away. "Would you stop trying to hurt me?"

His arm was bleeding and, cursing, he turned his back to me, striding towards the bathroom.

Silly boy. Turning his back on me. Probably because I'm a girl.

I jumped again, this time on his back. He yanked the pen out of his arm and turned with me clinging to him as best as possible.

I began to pound his back, his head, anywhere I could hit. He ran to the bed, twisting to fling me off him.

I landed on my belly and he quickly slammed his body against mine. His hand fisted my hair and he yanked, shoving me into the soft mattress at the same time.

I cried out in pain while simultaneously hating the thrill that went through me at his heavy weight on me. He jerked my head to the side, his lips coming down to press against my ear. "You don't seem to understand your position here."

I heaved against the mattress, clenching my fingers into the sheets. I hated, hated that the hair on my neck prickled at the feel of his breath washing over my skin.

The way my skin heated, the way his firm chest against my back made my insides squishy.

The position we were in was much too intimate. It reminded me of my last lover, how he used to whisper to me like this before he slid up inside me.

I blocked the image out, struggling to move my body out from under him and screamed out. "Get off!"

He chuckled darkly, jerking my hand towards the wall. It was too late when I realized that he'd cuffed one wrist to the bed.

He reached for my other hand and I turned quickly, raising

my knee at the same time. I got him straight in the balls, and he groaned, falling right on top of me.

Now I couldn't breathe, *the big lout.* He was so heavy.

I tried to shove him off me, but he was too strong and I only had one hand.

He recovered quickly and, moving too rapidly for my fighting body, he soon had my other wrist locked to the bed frame.

"Cheater." I kicked at him and he jerked backwards, his arm blocking my blow.

He scowled down at me. "Not a cheater."

He crawled off the bed, heading towards the bathroom.

"You are," I insisted, trying and failing miserably to jerk the cuffs off. At least they were lined with a soft material so they weren't too uncomfortable. "You said I was welcome to try and kill you."

"I'm not," he disappeared into the bathroom and, after a moment, the water came on, "a cheater."

While he was out of the room, I shifted, trying, and failing, for several minutes to figure out a way to get out of the cuffs.

He suddenly appeared in the doorway and I stilled, pretending I wasn't trying to saw the cuffs through the wooden frame. He'd taken off his jacket and shirt and had bandaged up his arm.

His eyes went straight to the cuffs and he smirked, as if knowing what I'd been trying to do. At the same time, I tried really hard not to stare at his chest.

And failed.

It was broad and expansive, and totally and completely ripped. Damn, he even had that sexy vee that dipped into his pants, and a trail of golden hair peeked out from--

I cut off the thought, suddenly realizing that he had several scars all over his chest, with three prominent ones in the middle.

I met his eyes, not wanting to think about what that might mean. "How can I kill you if I can't move from the bed?"

His smirk grew bigger. "That would be your problem. I never said I wouldn't cuff you."

I opened my mouth to protest but he disappeared into his closet, returning only a few minutes later with only a pair of sweatpants on and he headed straight for the bed.

Oh no. He wasn't planning on sleeping in the bed with me, was he? I spread out my arms and legs as far as they would possibly go, taking up as much space as possible. He came to stand over me, a frown gracing that sexy face.

"Sorry." I stared up at him, shrugging a shoulder. "No room for you."

He leaned down to within inches of my face. From here I could see flakes of yellow and dark brown in his golden eyes. They were incredibly stunning, and I could sense the barely restrained emotion he was holding back.

"Little baby nightmare, if you don't move your ass over, I will do it myself. Then I will tie up the rest of your body, positioned exactly the way that I want it, and I really don't think you would like that." He grinned, showing off his perfect smile that I hated so much.

"Say please, *mami*," I purred, and his smile fell. Heat filled his gaze and my throat was suddenly dry again.

Damn it.

Too much wine and no late-night snack. It was making me horny.

"How about this," his voice was a deep, sensual growl that did very bad things to my body. "I'll make a deal with you. You stop behaving like a brat, and I'll give you more freedom."

Hope sprung and my chest was tight with the thought. "Really?"

Dios, I sounded like a naive child but I couldn't help it.

He sighed, and leaned back on the bed, sitting down on the edge. He rubbed a hand over his face. He suddenly looked very tired. "Yes, Aster. I will."

"How about Rose? I want to see her."

He shook his head. "No. You're going to have to really behave if you want to see your sister."

"But, if I'm really really good, you'll try?"

"Maybe." He didn't look too confident about the sentiment.

"Promise me." I narrowed my eyes at him. "Swear it. On your mother's life."

He didn't answer right away, only stared at the floor. Finally, he tipped his head towards me. "My mom is dead, so no, I don't swear on her life."

I bit down on my lower lip, that old guilt resurfacing, even though I didn't want to feel bad for him. "What happened?"

His voice was flat and emotionless. "My father had her killed."

"Oh."

Shit. Maybe he wasn't as much like his father as I'd thought. A little bit of the hatred I had for him trickled out of me.

"I'm sorry."

He sighed heavily again and began to scoot me over. I let him. Laying next to me, he pulled the covers over both of us. "Don't worry about it, she wasn't a very attentive mother anyhow."

He turned on his side, his back to me, and I stared at him, trying to figure out what to do. "Do you want to talk about it?"

"No." He shook his head. "I want to sleep."

I didn't say anything, and suddenly the room descended into silence, except for the sound of the crickets outside. He began to snore softly, almost asleep within seconds. I shifted, trying to get comfortable but it was too hard with my wrists handcuffed to the bed.

"Prince Charming?" I suddenly, guiltily, realized I didn't know his real name.

"Stop calling me that," he growled.

"I would if I knew your name," I grumped back.

"It's Coulter."

"Fine," I tried to be polite, "*Coulter*, would you please unlock my handcuffs? I promise I won't try to kill you. Not tonight, anyhow."

He chuckled. "Not on your life."

"Please?" I shook my hips at him, trying to keep him awake. "With whipped cream and cherries on top?"

"I don't use whipped cream on naughty girls. Only good girls get the cream."

I swallowed down my response, not trusting my voice.

When I didn't answer him, he turned towards me, a scowl on his face. "Go to sleep, little nightmare."

I scowled back at him. "How come you get to call me Nightmare, but I can't call you Prince Charming?"

He shifted, sitting up to lean on his elbow, and I was overcome by the sexy, musky smell of him. Manly, like cedar and suede.

He lifted his hand to clip my jaw, his thumb coming up to part my lower lip as he leaned closer to me.

Oh, *Dios*. Was he going to kiss me?

My heart pitter-pattered, fluttering like a butterfly in my chest. Rouge marred my cheeks with arousal and my body stilled under his touch.

Digging my nails into the skin of my palms to keep myself grounded, I held my breath, my tongue coming out to lick over his thumb as I stared into impassioned, golden eyes.

Did I actually want him to kiss me?

He was so close now, close enough that he could easily brush his lips over mine.

"Because," he whispered, his cool breath washing over me. The scent of his musk marred my senses. "I'm neither a prince, nor charming." Tension strung my whole body tight, and it was only when he released my chin that I realized how much I'd wanted him to kiss me. Disappointment coiled in my stomach as he laid back down, turning away from me. Dismissing me. "Now go to sleep knucklehead, before I smother you with my pillow."

And, with that, he stilled, ignoring me. I tried to get comfortable, even though I was acutely aware of the heat of his body pressed to mine. It didn't take him long to fall asleep, and I hated the rejection burning inside me.

I closed my eyes, determining that I couldn't trust this man and his impossibly sexy looks. I shielded a wall up around my heart and forced myself to sleep, resolute to hate him with every core of my being.

SIX

Coulter

I WANTED TO KILL THAT LITTLE NIGHTMARE.

She drank my 49 Domaine Leroy wine. It had been Lily's favorite and the one I'd been saving up to share with her after I proposed. Then, after she died, I couldn't bring myself to drink it. I'd been tempted to smash it against the wall, so I'd shoved it under my bed, not wanting to destroy the symbol of our mutual love.

And when I'd walked in a few nights ago, with my room a crazy mess and her hair just as mussed...

She'd looked like a damn sexy siren, laid out on my bed with that bottle in her hand. Wine-stained, luscious lips pleading to be licked. Freckles on stark cheekbones, needing to be counted and kissed. One of my white shirts on, only half-way buttoned to show just enough of her tits to make my cock sit up and take notice. No friggin pants, and those damn sexy, tan, long legs that stretched for forever.

Then she opened her legs, a smirk on her face...

It took all my control to shut off the dirty thoughts racing through my mind.

The call of my dick, begging for some action.

The *invitation.*

To rip those silk pink panties off and drive right into her like a driller boring for oil.

Goddamn the fact that she was Rose's sister.

Otherwise, she'd be a great fuck. Something to distract my mind while I figured out all this shit I'd gotten into.

But right now, any Petrov female blood was off the table.

When Marisol had replaced my bandages, sniggering at my *pen* wound, I decided I would do whatever it took to get the nightmare under control and out of my hair. I had enough to worry about, and had zero time for troublemakers.

I'd spent the last several nights deep diving into my father's work, and had seen more violence in the past days than I had my whole life combined. I had to shut off all feelings just to make it through the long days . But at night, I was barely sleeping as those vicious images processed through my mind.

However, my father's doors began opening around me as I proved myself to him over and over. He either believed he could trust me, or he was too busy to question it further. He now took me with him every night, introducing me to all his current business partners. I'd quickly taken Bourbon's old place by his side, and I learned everything possible to gain an advantage over him.

On top of that, I was trying to broker an agreement with Nicholi, who was clearly holding a grudge that we'd killed Dimitri.

He was determined to make his cut of the drugs we sold bigger because of it, but I dug in my heels, demanding the same share we'd agreed to in the past.

I also couldn't get my mind off the blood my father drew from Bourbon. For once, I needed to be a step ahead of my father, and I now had a plan to learn the truth.

I just needed Aster to *behave* first before I could put it into action.

"Are you listening?" My father's angry voice snapped me back to the present and I nodded.

"Of course." I had an innate ability to hear almost everything around me, even when I wasn't completely focused on it. "Nicholi keeps insisting that we give him a higher price for the ozone, but I'm grinding him down. I'm using Dante's connections in Italy to dig up a weakness on him."

"Good." He nodded, not looking at me but staring out the window, watching the groups of people walking up and down the strip. It was nine o'clock, the beginning of Las Vegas nights. Crowds of happy people looking for a good time, while my father always seemed to be on the lookout for his next victim. "What about Posh?"

Posh was a new club we were opening. While we'd been gone, my father had bought one of the more popular clubs, completely gutted it, and was planning on a huge opening. It was my responsibility to plan the party.

"Fine," I waved his concern away, "I need to know about my uncle."

My father finally turned towards me, his eyes narrowed. "You don't need anything from me about Uncle Daimon. You should be the one giving me information. Have you gotten anything from him?"

My Uncle Daimon was the other man my father was keeping captive in the house, and that deeply disturbed me.

He'd been my father's consigliere for years and was a constant presence in my life. Dinners, vacations around the world, and late nights at the house with the family. He'd been even more present than my own father, and kinder too.

He mostly kept to himself, took his job seriously, and was never a problem. Unlike my other Uncle Crey, who was always blowing up relationships and causing chaos everywhere he went.

I clenched my jaw, not wanting to admit the truth. "It would help me if you told me how he fell out of favor with you."

Neither man was talking, and it was making extracting any information from Uncle Daimon extremely difficult. After greeting me with a hug and asking if Bourbon was still alive, my uncle hadn't said a single word more.

"You don't need to know that to get information from him," my father scoffed, tipping the rest of his glass of gin into his mouth, then slamming the empty glass down as the car came to a stop in front of the main club he owned, also where he conducted his shadier business.

"You coming tonight?" Brett opened his door and my father moved to climb out. "Romero is bringing a sample of his women to taste."

I pressed my lips in a firm line, trying to hold back my revulsion, but I couldn't suppress the shiver of disgust that crawled up my spine at the thought of being in the same room as my father, watching his orgy.

No fucking way in hell.

"No." I turned away, looking bored. "I have to speak to the Vitales tonight."

His eyebrows raised in surprise. "The Vitales?"

I gave him a curt nod. "Those are Dante's contacts."

"How does he know them?"

"Massimo Vitale is his cousin, twice removed."

My father studied me with newfound respect. The Vitales were ruthless mafia based out of Italy, and held a lot of power in our circle.

"Maybe you can arrange a meeting between us. The Kings can pick up their slack."

He was referring to the rumors that the Vitales had

tampered down on their sale of sex slaves. In fact, a whole ship-
ment of women had been discovered by the FBI at a port in
New York a couple of weeks ago, and the Vitales hadn't blinked
an eye.

And yet, even though they weren't trafficking as many
women, the Vitales still were ruthlessly driving out anyone
looking to fill in the gap, through any means, including
violence.

By the interest in my father's eyes, he was looking to pick
up the opening in the market, with their permission.

I leaned back in my seat and gave my father a cool look.
"Maybe."

My father's lips pressed into a firm line and he stared me
down. I could sense his rage and anger, unhappy that I wasn't
going to line up to his wishes like he'd expected.

I may have done so in the past, but the revelation that he'd
been raping Lily put a permanent wall between us.

He could fuck off, for all I cared.

The only reason I hadn't put a bullet in his brain was
because of the leverage he was holding over me.

Even though Bourbon and Rose were living outside of our
household, he still had Benny and his guards at their home,
watching over them to make sure they didn't escape.

He'd made it quite clear that, just as he was holding Aster
over Bourbon and Rose's head, their safety was his leverage
over me.

As the ire in his gaze landed on me, I expected him to fire
off a demand to obey him. Instead, his features calmed, his jaw
still grinding but his lips twisted upwards in a cruel smile.
"You've done well with Aster. I must admit, I wasn't sure if
you'd be able to keep her under control."

"Thank you." I was surprised by the compliment, and
strangely pleased. I hated the hum of pleasure that coursed

through me at his words, and I straightened my tie, newly bought and the same color as Aster's dress, to cover my reaction.

"If you can get the Vitales to the wedding, I'll allow you to bring the girl to see her sister, as long as you can guarantee that she'll be on her best behavior."

A terseness settled between us, as my father made his intentions known. The Vitales for the girl.

I knew that Rose was dying to see Aster, and, as much as I hated myself for it, I still wanted to give Rose everything she ever desired.

She was my soft spot, and my father knew it, dangling it over my head as often as possible.

"I'll see what I can do," I responded, not committing to anything. "But I want to start taking Aster out of the room."

He laughed, shaking his head. "You think you can control that woman?"

"I know I can." I didn't back down.

Still chuckling, he sighed. "I'll consider it. But if she escapes or does anything to harm us, it's your head on the line."

I nodded, agreeing to his terms.

"See that you get the Vitales to the wedding," my father pointed a finger at me, then he climbed out of the door and walked off without a goodbye or a backwards glance.

I waited only until after I saw him walk into the club then directed Brett back to the house.

I wasn't waiting for his approval. Time to put my plan in place.

SEVEN

Aster

I HEARD THE POUNDING OF FOOTSTEPS AND JUMPED OFF
the bed, rushing to the corner of the room. As soon as it opened,
I pounced, landing on someone's back.

Within seconds, I was shoved against the wall, a gun to my
head, with emotionless eyes boring into mine.

My tongue darted out, wetting suddenly dry lips, my hand
going to the one on my throat.

"Paranoid much?" I tried to grin at Coulter playfully,
ignoring the barrel pressed to my forehead. But I didn't look
away from his eyes, showing no fear, though the pulse at my
throat hammered in a panic.

His eyes, that beautiful golden color, were so cold. Hard.

Like a dead star.

He relaxed and tucked his gun back into his pants, but he
kept his hand on my throat, stepping closer to me. "Don't ever
do that again."

"If you were all that good of a guard, you would know that
there's no one else in here but me."

His gaze darkened. "I'm not a guard."

I reached forward, my finger grazing his cheekbone. "I know, you're a prince, and just as much a prisoner as I am."

I'd thought of his words the other night, about how his father had had his mother killed, and what it must've been like growing up with a father like that.

I'd decided to have a little bit of compassion.

His eyes grew even stonier, if possible. "I'm not a prisoner, so get any pretty thoughts about me being caught up in something I don't want to be a part of out of your head. I'm not your friend, and you being here means nothing to me. I'm following orders, that's it."

"Whatever you say, Prince Charming," I purred, stroking his wrist with my thumb.

He stepped back, letting me go, putting space between us as he took in the room, which I'd cleaned in my effort to behave better. "You cleaned."

"You're observant." I huffed. "Why are you here, then, if you don't care about me?"

"I'm making sure my little nightmare captive is still here."

I frowned, hating his cocky grin. "You already knew that, Marisol was just in here, talking my ear off."

"You're right. She told me you cleaned your mess." He nodded his head at the room. "You kept up with your end up the deal. I'm here to keep up with mine."

"What's that mean?" I tilted my head to study him, trying to smother the hope planting itself into my chest like a seed trying to take root.

"I'm taking you out."

"Really?!" It was too late. Hope filled my chest, digging itself into my heart and shooting out roots. Overjoyed, I jumped into his arms, unable to stop myself. Surprisingly, he caught me, and didn't let go. I wrapped my legs around his waist and leaned back to look into his face, grinning. "You're going to take me to see Rose?"

He frowned and shook his head. "I didn't say that."

"But—" I tried to protest.

"You have to earn more of my trust to see your sister."

I studied those golden eyes, feeling the heat of my attraction for him flush up my chest. Once again, I was overwhelmed with his smell, the mop of his gorgeous hair, the sadness in his eyes, despite his words.

I was a sucker for tortured men; I understood them much more than I wanted to.

Scowling, I grit my teeth, forcing down any kind of affection for the man. I didn't like this prick. And I shouldn't be so happy he was taking me out of the room.

I wasn't a Stockholm victim.

"All right," I responded simply, not wanting to give an inch, though I wasn't stupid. He had all the power and I knew it. I thrust my hand upwards, like a knight commanding her army. "Take me out and let's see what happens."

He sighed, shaking his head, then set me on my feet. "First, I have conditions."

I frowned. "What conditions?"

Letting go of my waist, he pulled something out of his pocket, and my scowl deepened. "I'm *not* wearing that."

"If you want out of this house, you'll have to wear it. Plus, you'll have to hide in the back seat."

I jerked the black , silk-lined bag from his fingers and put it over my own head, hating it. At least it smelled nice. "And how am I supposed to walk with this thing over my head?"

"You're not." Grabbing my hips, he jerked me off my feet and threw me over his shoulder. "And don't say a word, or I'll lock you up in the basement."

THE LAST TIME I'd been this mortified was when I had to sneak back into the house after losing my virginity to Jose Varga at the awesome age of sixteen.

It'd been out in the barn, and my hair was full of hay, my clothes tussled, my inner thighs sticky with his come. My embarrassment and disappointment marked my face as I'd scurried in through the back entrance, sneaking down the hallways and past my Papa's room.

Since then, sex had become much better than Jose's clumsy attempts to deflower me, but I'd never forgotten the shame I'd felt, hiding that from my Papa.

And now, I was scrunched down into the back of Coulter's back seat, the sound of his loud engine roaring in my ears. Coulter drove a sleek, black refurbished 1970 Remi Cuda, the updates so new, the leather seats still had that new car smell.

I'd yanked the bag off my face, thinking it ridiculous, but I was quiet as we'd left through the gates of his house and onto the busy Las Vegas streets.

After several minutes, Coulter parked the car but he didn't move, just stared out the front window, and I couldn't help but wonder what he was thinking about.

The sounds from the busy city were muted—we were at the back end of a parking deck, and the silence seemed to stretch forever.

"If you're not quiet, I will have to force you to do something you're not going to like." His startling, cold words sent a shiver up my spine and an angry outburst from my mouth.

"I didn't even make a peep. Not even after we left your house."

"You were good the whole way here, and that's the only reason I'm trusting you now." He still didn't look at me. "But this is your warning. If you try to run off, or misbehave in any way, you're not going to like the repercussions."

I struggled to squeeze myself out from the floor of the back seat, until finally, I could sit up enough to stare at his profile.

He really was a beautiful man. His features sharp, perfectly carved like an Adonis statue or a di Vinci.

One of those pieces of art that stole your breath the minute you looked at it. And if you stared at it for too long, your chest began to ache with a longing that would never go away. Yet, you continued to stare, wishing you could will it into existence, into a living, breathing creature.

"Where are we?"

He finally turned, his sharp profile becoming 3D, melding before my very eyes. And yet, his gaze was still harsh, his eyes flat and emotionless. "Somewhere you're not going to like."

It was like pressing my face against the side of an ice statue, staring into those eyes. Goosebumps skirted up my arms and prickled the hair at the back of my neck. "Then why did you bring me here?"

"So that you'll exactly understand your situation. My father has kept you in the house, treated you fairly well. That's because Rose and Bourbon insisted on it. But I need you to know, Aster, my father is not a nice man, and the sooner you know this, the better off your life will be."

My throat was suddenly full. "And are you?"

He raised an eyebrow. "Am I what?"

"A nice man?"

His eyes lowered from mine to take in my face. They lingered over my hair and cheekbones, to my nose, then landed on my lips. "No."

"Then why should I do what you ask?"

"Because, my little nightmare," his voice was mocking as he

leaned in, and his scent trailed over me like silk, caressing my senses. "You want to."

I frowned, suddenly realizing that I'd tilted my face towards him, my whole body responding as if silently begging him to touch me. There was an amusement in his eyes, and a cockiness to his gaze that said he knew exactly how much I wanted to do what he asked.

"You wish, Prince Charming." Pushing the passenger seat down, I jerked the door open. I crawled out, awkward and clumsy, wishing his car wasn't so cramped. When I was finally free, I straightened, flipping my hair back. "Now, show me what a terrible man your father is." I spoke with a dry sarcasm but my stomach twisted, having the feeling that I wasn't going to like what he showed me.

Shaking his head, he chuckled under his breath and slid smoothly out his own door. I met him by his door, and he lightly placed the palm of his hand on the small off my back, guiding me through the parking deck to a side door of the building. A tall, Hispanic-looking man was standing guard outside it and Coulter approached him.

"Carlos. You didn't see her, you understand?"

Carlos only nodded once before staring behind us, ignoring us as Coulter used his key card to open the door. Grabbing my wrist, he led me down several dimly lit hallways until we entered a small room.

He didn't turn the light on, but he didn't need to for me to see a few monitors set up on a large, cheap-looking table.

They were already on and, after gesturing for me to sit, I saw that we were looking through a video feed.

The screens were focused on busy hallways, people at gambling tables, and also private rooms filled with people playing more intimate games. "Shouldn't security be here?" I asked him.

He waved me off. "There's additional security upstairs."

"What are we here for, then?"

"Patience, little nightmare." Reaching forward, he flipped on a new screen. "Scoot over."

The screen was slow to warm up, then it took a moment for me to understand what I was seeing, but when I did, I inhaled a sharp breath, my hand going to my mouth. "Is that what I think it is?"

"Depends on what you think it is." He was doing that thing where he wasn't looking at me again. Instead, he focused on the screen, a dull look in his eyes.

There was a room full of people and it looked like a full on orgy was happening. Except, it wasn't what I would consider a normal orgy.

There was blood everywhere.

Though the room was dimly lit, I could see it sparkle. On the floor, in the clothing, in people's hair.

Women far outnumbered the men, and my stomach churned with the cuffs and chains wrapped around their wrists and ankles. There were some women on their hands and knees, with a dick in their mouth and another in their ass. There were also whips involved, as well as knives.

I caught the look on one of the women's face, and even from my safe place perched behind the screen, I could see the deadness in her eyes.

These women were not here willingly.

There was also a man in the center of the room, tied to a chair. Black liquid spilled from his neck, staining his shirt. He was slumped over. If he wasn't dead now, he would be soon.

"I didn't know it was going to be this bad." Coulter's voice had an edge to it, and disgust etched his perfect features, revealing genuine emotion. "I'm sorry I brought you here."

I was taken back by his apology. I pointed to the man tied to the chair, not knowing how to react to it. "Who is that?"

He frowned. "That's Mark Williams. He used to work for us."

"Did you know they were going to kill him?"

He faced me. "I told you, Aster. I'm not a good man. This man stole from my father, and no one does that and lives."

I met his eyes with a determined gaze. "I will never let you take advantage of me that way." I gestured to the screen with my hand. "I will kill myself before anyone fucks me like that."

His hand snapped out and he grabbed my wrist again, this time, digging his fingers in so that his nails bit into my skin. His eyes were fiercely intense. "I will never let anyone use you like that."

"But those girls, how can you let them--"

"I can't help those girls. But I can help you, Aster. I swear I didn't know it was going to be like this." He straightened, his hand still clinched on my wrist. "But I did know it was going to be bad. I needed you to see this because, if you continue to fight me, then it will make it that much harder for me to protect you."

"And will you? Protect me?"

His eyes held mine. "I swear that I'll protect you, Aster. Even if I have to kill my own father to do it."

"But why?" I suddenly felt weak and useless. "Why are you protecting me?"

"Because." His throat bobbed, and his thumb brushed over my wrist. Softly, almost absentmindedly, but it sent my heart racing. "I couldn't help your sister when she needed it, and I swore I would never do that again."

"Rose?" I was suddenly panicked. "Is she okay? What's happening—"

"Not Rose." His voice was suddenly a dark growl. "Your other sister."

My heart pounded in my chest and the pure vitriol he exuded. Now I saw everything, the spectrum of emotions he'd been holding back. Pain. Rage. Anger. Passion.

"Lily." My throat was dry. I'd met her when I was really little and didn't remember much about her. I hadn't even known she was my sister when I met her.

He nodded.

"What happened to her?"

His gaze darkened. "She's dead. And I'm going to kill the man who killed her."

"Who is that?"

Coulter leaned in. "Aster, do you understand now that if you continue to fight me, my father might try to make you become like one of those women?" His fingers on my wrist were digging into it harshly. "If you fight me, I will still protect you, because that's a promise I've made to Rose. But you need to help me help you."

I remembered the dead look on that girl's face. The blood running from that man's throat. The dead look in Coulter's eyes in the car.

Could I truly trust him? What if he turned on me, too?

He said he made a promise to Rose, but what if it was just a manipulation to make his life easier?

"Are you going to help me escape?"

"There is no escape for you, now. The quicker you learn this, the easier it will be for you to accept it."

"But. Why?"

"What do you know about your parents? Do you know the truth about your heritage?"

I nodded. "I'm from Russia, the mafia. My Papa told me— after Lily died..."

"You've lived a good life, Aster. Your childhood was free

and innocent. But my father drug you back into this world, and now, you'll never get out of it."

"But," I stared into his eyes, wishing his grip on my wrist wasn't so tight. It felt like shackles, suffocating and smothering. "What if I don't want to be in this world?"

"Do any of us?"

The room was silent, closing in on me even more.

"Why then, why keep me safe?"

"I told you. I made a promise to Rose. Besides, the faster you're out of my hair, the easier it'll be to get what I want."

Out of his hair. Like a piece of lint. Or hay, annoying and telling of something dirty. "Which is what?"

"Revenge."

The coldness was back in his gaze, and I had no doubt that 'revenge' meant murder.

His ability to switch his emotions on and off at the flip of a switch had my stomach churning. I couldn't trust this man.

"I need to see Rose."

He suddenly let me go, sighing, and ran his hand through his golden hair. When he released his hand, a lock of hair was in his face.

I wanted to reach up and brush it away. There was a sadness in his eyes that made me want to feel bad for him.

Again, I was switching on and off from feeling compassionate to feeling mistrust, and it was driving me crazy.

Where I'd come from, I knew my place in the world and how to exist in it.

Here, I was torn between my natural inclination to care, and the need to survive.

"Aster, I promise you that Rose is happy."

"I don't believe you. I need to see it with my own eyes."

"You will see her at her wedding."

"Her wedding? That's too late. What if she wants to escape?"

"Trust me, she *wants* to marry my brother."

"I can't trust you. Not until I see with my own eyes."

"Fine." He stood up, looming over me like a dark shadow. "If you help me, then I will take you to your sister."

I jumped to my feet, meeting his gaze. "Before her wedding?"

"Before her wedding." He held out his hand, and I took it, shaking it, feeling like I was making a promise to the devil to save my sister.

If I'd only known how much it was the truth.

EIGHT

Coulter

I HUNG UP THE PHONE, HAVING JUST ARRANGED A NEW contract for a popular fragrance company to launch its new brand at the opening of Posh.

Now, I sat at my desk, my palms laid flat, with three burner phones in between them, and tried to get the image of what I'd just seen on that screen off of my mind.

I hadn't wanted to take Aster there, and yet, I'd felt like I needed her to see, to know what she, what *we*, were up against.

But goddamn, I hated the look on her face when she understood what was happening. It's like I could see the innocence draining from her...

I regretted showing her now; there were other things I could've done that weren't so revolting.

The dead man in the middle of the room--no surprise. I'd known for a while now that his days were up.

The orgy of dead eyed women--not happy about it, but not a surprise either.

But the blood...the room was bathed in it.

I knew my father was sick but that level of sickness...

I wasn't one to kink-shame but to not only rape women, but to also hurt them like that when you did it... it was nauseating. Unforgivable.

My heart was racing, my breathing so harsh, I even registered the sound in my own ears. I was losing it, and here I was, just sitting here like a lump of fucking coal, doing nothing.

Did I rush in there to stop it? No.

Useless.

I disgusted myself.

I also hated how cold I was already becoming, but it was necessary.

It took a hard man to kill his own father.

"So. What's next?"

Dante's harsh tone snapped me out of my thoughts. My face moved to his but his eyes were on my desk. Without knowing it, I'd grabbed a phone and was crushing it into my hands. I forced myself to relax, letting go of it. Flexing my fingers, I leaned back in my seat to stare at Dante and Knight, who sat on the sofa across from my desk.

My office was urban themed, with dark grey concrete floors, and brick walls painted a light grey. An expensive Italian rug was placed over the floor, 'hiding' one of our many vaults.

My desk wasn't an expensive one. It was actually an old one I'd found at one of our warehouses but I liked it, wondering who had put the knife gashes into it.

"Now that I've gained my father's trust, it's time to implement my plan."

"Which is what?" The sweet smell of Knight's blunt filled my nose. He'd been doing that more and more now, ever since he'd escaped from Russia.

"Part one. Find out what my father is doing with Bourbon's blood." I pulled a lighter from my pocket and began to flick it, watching the flame spark and burn out.

"You haven't figured that out yet?" Knight exhaled, and the smoke hung in the air, masking his facial expression.

I shook my head. "The doc's staying tight-lipped about it. I don't want to push her too hard, or she may tell my father that I've been asking. I've looked into everything I could about her, as well as anything that might connect her father to mine." I shook my head. "Nothing. She's too well connected to find anything useful."

"She's from our world." Knight said.

I stopped flicking the lighter to look up at him. "How so?"

"We have the same history, except she hides hers."

"She has Cuban mafia blood?"

Knight nodded, his bloodshot eyes half lidded.

"How do you know that?" I hadn't been able to find any connection to the mafia world at all.

"How else do you think I know? Some things I just know."

I nodded, my eyes focusing on the lighter again but the gears in my mind were moving. It was true, Knight's family had been deeply embedded in the mafia for generations and generations. With that, came knowledge about the old ways that the newer generations wouldn't have.

If it was true, which it probably was, then she had gone to great lengths to hide her identity. And somehow, my father had found out.

"Okay, so it's either connected to that, or to something personal."

"Or both," Dante said.

I nodded. "Or both."

"So if the doctor's not opening up, how are you going to figure it out?" Knight asked.

"I'm going to use Aster." I tilted my head towards the bathroom where Aster and Candi were talking; I'd called in Candi to help get Aster ready for what I needed tonight.

Dante scoffed. "She's not going to help you."

"I know she will."

"And I know she's unpredictable. You can't trust her."

Knight nodded. "That girl will tell the doctor everything, just to spite you."

"Or for fun." Dante agreed.

I shook my head. "I don't think so. Not after tonight."

"Why don't you use one of our girls? One we know is loyal to us. Candi would be perfect for the job."

"Because Candi can easily be connected to us. Aster can't."

They both fell silent at this, nodding, and I pulled my cell from my pocket and texted John, the guy I had tailing the doctor, verifying her location.

"Okay," Candi's chipper voice interrupted our silence, "she's ready."

Aster stepped out from the bathroom, and even from where I sat, I could see the anger flashing in her eyes. "I'm not going anywhere in this outfit."

I leaned back in my chair, my fingers frozen on my lighter as I stared at the sexual creature in front of me. She was wearing a push-up bra and bikini bottom, with a leather strappy top across her chest and knee-high stiletto boots.

Her dark smokey eyes and all black outfit was a gorgeous contrast to her fiery red hair that fell in sexy waves down her back.

She was my fucking wet dream come to life.

My dick lurched, hardening in my pants at the sight of her.

I glanced at Knight and Dante, who were both staring at her with heated gazes.

I wanted to gouge their eyes out. They shouldn't be looking at her like that.

I forced down the jealousy boiling under the surface

because, as much as Aster's sensuality made my dick hard, I couldn't do anything about it.

She was Rose's sister.

Lily's sister.

I wasn't touching that bloodline with a ten foot pole, and the sooner I could get her out of my life, the better.

In fact, even better if one of my best friends took her off my hands.

I tormented myself with the image of her kissing both Dante and Knight, writhing in their laps as they took her together.

I tortured myself more with the image of Rose and Bourbon kissing next to them, knowing my life would be a living hell if I allowed that to happen.

"Get your fucking eyes off her," I growled at my men, and both their faces immediately snapped to mine.

Dante's eyes narrowed. "What the fuck, boss?" He knew I was determined to get rid of her as soon as possible.

Knight only smirked and, leaning back in his chair, he took another drag of his blunt. When he was done, he opened his mouth to respond but didn't get a chance, as Aster stormed across the room in her six-inch stilettos towards me.

"I think all King men must have a hearing problem. I told you I'm not going anywhere in this."

"You are." I gave her a cool look then, reaching into my desk, I pulled out the collar I'd picked out, just for her. Standing, I walked around my desk towards her. "Turn around."

"In your dreams." She reached behind her to undo the straps across her chest. I shoved the collar in my pocket, then grabbed her arm, stopping her.

"If you want to work with me, instead of against me, you'll do exactly what I say."

She scowled up at me.

Growling, I maneuvered her back into my chest, then wrapped my fingers around her stomach, pulling her tight to me. Could she feel my halfway hard-on? "You will do this, Aster, because it will help your sister." I nipped at her ear, my breath moving over her shoulder.

She stilled, her hands still on the strap at the nape of her neck. "I'm practically naked."

"You're sexy." Unable to stop myself, I leaned back and ran a knuckle down her back, following the line of muscle. God, her skin was so silky. "You'll be able to get any man or woman to do whatever you want."

She closed her eyes, leaning her head back against my chest. "Is that what you want me to do?"

My eyes followed the spattering of freckles that flared down her neck, her back arching, her breasts pressing outward. My fingers itched to pull down that black velvet bra, to see what her freckled tits would look like spilling from it. "I want you to trust me."

Suddenly aware that everyone was staring at us, my hand on her belly tightened. I grit my teeth. "Candi, give me her coat."

"No."

I turned to stare at her. "What did you say?"

"Aster doesn't deserve to be treated like this." Candi's hands were on her hips, and a red blush spread out across her face, growing deeper as my scowl at her disobedience grew fiercer.

Candi had never spoken to me this way. We'd always had a great relationship. She kept an eye on the girls in the clubs, giving me any information I might need to know about them and the people who walked in. And when I came in to the club she worked at, I would often stay late, using my experience to help her understand the ins and outs of owning a small business—on her off time, she made jewelry and sold it online.

But now, by the fierceness of her gaze, I could see that Aster had gotten to her. They'd only spent minutes together and yet, she was feeling defensive of Aster. This not only revealed how dangerous taking Aster out could be, but also that Aster wasn't on my side. Not yet.

Still holding Aster close, my scowl turned into a dangerous look. "And how am I treating her?"

"Like a hooker."

"And you, you know more than I do about my own business?"

"I know she's dressed up like one."

"When have I ever forced a girl to do something against her will?"

"Never." She took a nervous step back, shaking her head. Aster turned around and put her hand on my arm, her heat seeping through my shirt.

"Coulter," her voice was low and soft, full of the same sweetness that Rose exuded. The kind that slowly curled and twisted around your heart until it choked it of life. "It's okay, I'll go."

Pulling Aster to my side, I stepped closer to Candi and leaned down to stare straight into her eyes. "Not that it's any of your business, but what I'm *forcing* Aster to do, very well may save her life."

At this, Candi's throat bobbed, her face paling. "Okay."

My other hand snapped out and pulled her to me so that we were inches apart. I tried not to let the rage I was feeling inside overtake me. "Don't ever question me again, is that clear?"

She nodded, and I softened my hold over her arm to put my hand on her shoulder, squeezing it softly. "I swear Candi, I'm only trying to do what's right here."

"You're changing."

"I have no choice but to change."

She stared at me a moment longer, her throat bobbing. "Just don't become like him."

My father.

"I will never make that promise."

It was already too late.

NINE

Aster

I was hella uncomfortable. Not only were my boobies popping out of this tight velvet bra, but the panties were riding up my ass.

"What are we doing?" I hated being in the dark about everything. I trusted Coulter enough to be in the car with him right now but the images of those girls on the screen had my stomach cramping.

"I need you to do something for me."

I crossed my hands across my chest and turned to stare at him. "I'm not fucking someone."

He glanced at me, a half smile on his face. "That's not the kind of favor I'm talking about."

"Then what?"

"I'll tell you when we get there."

"Why?" I gripped the car door handle, considering jumping out. We were stuck in the middle of downtown Vegas traffic, and cars lined up in front of us at the stoplight.

"Because." Coulter reached forward and grasped my chin,

turning my face towards him. "Aster, be a good girl and trust me."

I snapped my teeth at his fingers, catching one in between them. I bit it softly. "I don't like being a good girl."

"Then pretend you can behave until I can trust you enough to bring you to Rose."

"Maybe you're the one who needs to learn to trust me and just tell me right now." I wrapped my tongue around his finger and pulled it into my mouth, sucking on it.

Why I couldn't stop myself from flirting with him was beyond me.

His face jerked towards mine, his eyes landing on my lips, where they sat, frozen.

He tasted forbidden. The shadowed man leading his little *nightmare* to hell.

He sighed and pulled his finger from my hold but, instead of putting it back on the steering wheel, he wiped my saliva across my lips. I flicked my tongue out, tasting his finger again but he lowered his hand to my neck, wrapping fingers around it. His thumb sat on the knot of my throat, pressing there.

I tilted my head upwards, allowing it. Inviting it.

There was something so dominant about him when he did that to me.

It commanded my attention, demanded my obedience.

It also made my heart race.

I liked it.

"Tell me." I stared into those beautiful, troubled eyes, demanding the truth. "Why am I dressed up like this?"

"I need you to seduce the truth from someone."

"I said—"

"I said seduce, not fuck."

"Who?"

"A woman. She's a doctor, and an up and coming Nevada

senator's wife. She has information I need, and you're going to get it from her."

A doctor and *a senator's wife?* "Seriously? Me?" I was all for using sex appeal to get what I wanted, but I'd never tried it on a woman before.

I was trying to ignore the feel of his palm across the sensitive pulse of my throat and the way it made my cheeks flush.

Thank God it was dark out.

"Yes." *Squeeze.* "You."

"Yeah, I'm not doing that." I put my hand over his, slowly lowering it from my neck, and turned away from those golden eyes that captivated me. Instead of arguing with me, Coulter parallel parked in between two cars, then turned off the car.

I stared out the window, watching the people crowded around a man drawing on the sidewalk with chalk. I watched him curiously, trying not to think about the tension filling the car.

"I think you will, Aster." Coulter's voice was calm and confident. "I think you will, because you need to do it for your sister."

"You keep saying that." I jerked my head back and twisted in my seat towards him, narrowing my eyes. "Maybe you're lying just to get me to do what you want."

He shook his head, the golden mop of hair fell into his face. My cheeks heated again as Coulter's hand went to my shoulder, his finger tracing softly over my collarbone. "I'm not lying."

He traced his finger down my collar to the swell of my breast.

Pressed against Coulter's warm body at night, handcuffed to the bed, I'd had a sex dream about him last night. The image of him hovering over me flashed through my mind, the thought of him sliding in and out of me while I was still tied to the bed, helpless to stop him. I was growing wet just thinking about it.

This man was dangerous. Too goddamn sexy for his own good.

I flicked my tongue out, wetting suddenly dry lips. "Then tell me, what's it for? How will this help Rose?"

I couldn't see his eyes, they were shrouded in the darkness of the car, but his finger continued to travel in between my breasts, making my nipples perk.

"When Rose, Bourbon, my brother, and I arrived, my father took some of Bourbon's blood. You're going to find out what he's going to do with it. You're going to convince the doctor to tell you what."

I sucked in a breath as his finger began to move down to my stomach towards the vee of my thighs. "And how am I supposed to do that, when even you couldn't?"

"By now, she'll be drunk. Buzzed, at least." A shoulder came up. "Her husband's asked for a woman for his wife. You're a woman. Seduce her enough to get her to open up to you."

"I don't know if I could do that to a woman."

"If she's into women, you can. Even if she's not..." His hand moved to my side, his fingers wrapping around my waist. He finally looked up, staring into my eyes as he slowly pulled me towards him. "You're beautiful, Aster. Sensual. My own personal nightmare."

My cheeks burned at his compliment and I pretended like his words didn't make me purr inside like a kitty. "Why wouldn't the doctor tell you what she's doing with it?"

"You would make my life easier if you just obeyed orders without asking questions." He leaned in, cedar and suede and musk filling my nose.

I stared into gorgeous eyes. "I'm not one of your little minions."

His nose brushed over mine. "No, you're my little she-devil, come to torture me."

His lips caressed my skin, nipping right next to my mouth, and I closed my eyes, overcome by the sensation of him. His masculine smell filled my nose. The whisper of his lips spread heat across my chest and a tingle in between my thighs. I was drowning in everything Coulter, unable to come up for air. "And yet, I'm your prisoner, instead of the other way around."

He stilled, then pulled back. "No more questions. It's time. Take off your coat."

I opened my eyes; he was back to the hardened man I was very familiar with. He reached into his pocket, pulling out a strange looking set of handcuffs, this time with a longer chain between the two cuffs, and what looked like a grown up version of a dog collar. "Do as I instruct, and we just may save your sister."

THE CLUB WAS CROWDED, the music so loud that it vibrated through my body like a pulsing, pounding heartbeat.

The air smelled of smoke and lust, coated with sweat and lascivious appetite.

Coulter led me by a chain, one end attached to his wrist, the other to the collar at my neck.

He'd explained that this was one of his father's *special* clubs, where back rooms were paid for with hefty fees and taciturn discretion, and that the collar was a form of protection for me.

We made our way through the crowded dance floor, the air hazy with infused smoke and red lights, like the mouth of hell opening up before me. A pit of nervousness grew in my stomach but I continued onward, encouraged by the tugging at my throat.

Coulter led me through wandering corridors and rooms, until finally, we entered a back hallway.

Darkness shrouded over me like a wet, suffocating blanket and I pulled in a sucking breath, trying to see Coulter's golden mop of hair ahead of me. Blobs of black filled the edges of my vision, the tugging at my collar still insistent, the only thing keeping my feet moving, one after the other.

The deeper I traveled into the belly of this underworld, the more intense the mood became. Fingers tickled my arms and legs, growing more bold. The darkness was too thick, the air too smothering. I couldn't make Coulter out in the darkness. I couldn't see anything.

Hands grew more insistent, grappling at my breasts and ass, lewd whispers pressed in my ear. Bodies packed tight against me, forcing me into a wave of indiscernible movement.

Fear sparked, smothering my lungs in a layer of cotton, panic crawling up my throat. "Coulter!"

My panicked words immediately dissolved in the chaos of the sweat and hunger surrounding my senses.

The cuff at my neck still urged me forward and I stumbled, trying to follow the unknown path as he urged me forward.

"Come to have a good time, little kitten?" A presence pressed into my side, a low, coarse voice in my ear. I couldn't see him, but I could feel his fingers sliding down my bare back.

"No, thank you."

There were rules here, of that I was sure.

Safe, sane, and consensual.

"That's not the safe word." Hands slid up over my ass, tugging my bottom with it and baring my flesh to the open air of the club. Lips pressed against my jaw as fingers trickled towards the space between my thighs. "You feel incredible, pussycat."

I froze in panic, my terror making my feet like lead.

I couldn't speak; invisible claws tightened around my throat.

The only sound in my ears was my own heartbeat, pounding harshly in time to my rapid breathing.

The tugging at my neck turned into a harsh pull, jerking me out of my frozen state and into a firm chest. Fingers twisted into the collar, cutting off my air, stopping my panicked breathing. "Can't you see she's taken, asshole?"

The smell of cedar and suede surrounded my senses, overcoming the sweat and lust-filled air, replacing it with a warm and comforting feeling.

Safety.

I didn't need my sight to know that it was Coulter.

He affirmed it with his low growl by my ear, his fingers tugging on the collar at my throat. "Get the fuck away before I cut your dick off."

"Oh shit, man. I'm sorry." The same voice who, only a moment earlier had been coarse and crude, defended. "I can't see shit in here."

"Then you need to get your eyes checked." Coulter growled again. Wrapping his arm around my waist, he pulled me away, not acknowledging the man's apology. As he hauled me off, his words echoed through the chambers of my mind.

Get your eyes checked...Get your eyes checked...

The hum of safety I'd felt at his reappearance dissipated, the sound of his derision reverberated through the skeleton of my body, clinking against bone after bone after bone.

Get your eyes checked.

Something I'd failed to do and was now paying the consequences for it.

Panic clawed at my throat again, tears rolling down my cheeks. *I was losing my sight, with only a slight chance of gaining it back.*

I had a genetic disease affecting my retinas. It would eventually affect my eyesight to the point where I would never see the sun in the blue sky, the twinkle of city lights, the bright colors of the flowers in a garden.

With losing my sight, I was also losing the very thing that connected me to my mother: our gardening together. It was almost as if I was losing her for the second time.

I was suddenly drowning.

A sinking mermaid in the depths of the inferno's fiery ocean.

As we moved, Coulter clutched me so tight that there was no space between me and the prince leading me through his kingdom. It was only because of this that I made my way through the crowd.

Get your eyes checked.

As he sat me down, I choked on a sob, my fingers clutched to my chest. Nails digging into my skin, pain striking like lightning, I tried to force my mind into the present. *This isn't the place for that.*

"Aster." A demanding voice in my ear, but a gentle grip on my arm. "Aster." Fingers went to my throat, not squeezing, but grounding me. "Take in a deep breath, baby." Pain sparked on my thigh, wrenching me to the present. I sucked in a choking breath, and though it felt like sandpaper over my ribs and lungs, I could suddenly breathe.

I blinked and the panicked blackness at the edges of my vision slowly subsided, revealing dim grey and red light shrouding the room.

Deep golden eyes stared into mine.

Grounding me.

"Coulter." My voice choked and I blinked several times, only now registering the concern in his eyes. Gone was the cold, the stoniness of his gaze. In its place, was a man, kneeling between my legs, worry in his gaze.

"Aster, what's wrong?"

I looked away, staring into the dark grey of the club and didn't answer.

I wanted to believe that he actually cared but fear made me press my lips into a firm line, closing up. I never spoke to anyone about my anxiety attacks. "Nothing Coulter. Is she here?"

Suddenly, his fingers clasped my cheeks, turning my face roughly towards him. His molten gaze was back.

"What," he ground the word out, "happened?" The intensity of his concern softened something inside me but the experience of my past played like a broken record in my mind.

Men only cared when you were fun.

Carefree and happy.

Playing the character that they saw and liked in you, like a wide-eyed, cheerful Barbie, with no sadness or pain.

Anxiety attacks or panicking wasn't *convenient* to their schedules.

They had no emotional space for dealing with something like that.

And a man like Coulter, who could switch his emotions on and off like a light switch...I couldn't open up to a man like that.

We were also in the middle of the club, and he was expecting me to get answers from the doctor.

I swallowed down the words I wanted to say, the burden I'd carried for too long, and lied. "I told you. Nothing."

"Are you sure?" His fingers looped through mine and he pressed the knuckles to his lips, kissing them softly. "You can talk to me."

I wavered, touched, tears sparking my eyes as relief flooded through me. I wanted to open up to him, to show him all the dark and ugly parts inside me.

But I couldn't.

I was still too guarded and afraid.

I replaced the openness on my face with the mask I often wore, closing off my emotions and quickly wiping away my tears. "I'm okay, Coulter. Really." He gave me a skeptical look, so I rushed to find an explanation. "That guy just freaked me out." I smiled, touching his face. "Thank you, but I'm okay now. Is the doctor here?"

His eyebrows furrowed as his eyes traced over my face. His lips pursed but, after a moment, his fingers relaxed and he looked away, releasing me from his hold. He straightened, sitting on a chair next to me. Wrapping one arm around my waist, he pointed back in the direction of a hallway. "She's in that room."

I turned and narrowed my gaze, trying to see what he wanted me to see. "Where?"

"See that row of private rooms?" I nodded, and he continued. "There's only one with someone standing guard."

"Okay," I nodded, part relieved that he hadn't persisted, the other part of me disappointed. Insistence meant that someone actually cared enough to press me into telling them my truth.

I stood up, stumbling a little on my spiked black heels. With firm hands on my hips, Coulter caught me, balancing me, and I leaned into his steadying touch, taking a deep breath to refocus myself. I dug my nails into my palms, letting the warmth of his hands on my hips soothe my inner demons until I felt a calming center.

"I'm going." I pushed away, walking towards the room on steady feet.

As I approached, the man guarding the doorway seemed to

grow larger. He had a chest as thick as a large tree, arms bulging like small boulders at his side. He was relaxed, as if he was a little bit bored but, at my approach, he tensed, his eyes sharp as they took me in.

He did a thorough once over, not taking in my bikini bottoms or my boobs busting out of my top, but at my legs and hips, underarms, as if looking for a weapon. It was a short check, as I literally had few places to hide anything.

When I stopped in front of him, he stared me down with a stony glare. He didn't attempt conversation, just waited for me to speak.

"Chocolate spice cake." I told him the password that Coulter gave me in the car.

His stance immediately relaxed but his eyes swept over my face, studying me. Once he was done with his second assessment, he stepped to the side and opened the door.

I passed the silent muscle bound dude and stepped into the room. Coulter told me that he would be observing us through a hidden camera feed, though no one else knew about it. I wondered if he'd already pulled out his phone and was watching, waiting to see what I would do.

Grinning at all the ways I could fuck with him, I strode into the room, taking in everything around me.

The room was laid out like a bedroom, with a high, platform bed featured in the center, and sensual, black and white photos framed over it. A plush, blue velvet sofa rested against the black, bricked wall and a crystal chandelier hung from molded ceiling tiles. Blue lights softened the view before me: a naked man on the bed. He was on his knees, with one man fucking him in his mouth and another in his ass.

Even in his position, I recognized him from the picture Coulter had shown me. He was the doctor's husband, and running for a Senate seat in the next election.

Just for fun, I thought about joining the three men on the bed, only to see how Coulter would react. Clamping down on my smile, I walked deeper into the room.

There was a table on the side, where a lone woman sat, watching them. She was fully dressed, with a tight, white business dress that had a deep cut, making her boobies pop out. Her hair was pulled back into a tight pony tail and she had on glasses. She had the whole, sexy librarian look down pat.

From where I stood, I could only see her profile, but her eyes were riveted on the men on the bed.

It was only when I walked closer that I could see her clearly. Her back was ramrod straight and she held a wine glass to her lips. Not drinking it but only pressing it there. In fact, her lips were closed, pressed into a firm line. A mixture of sadness and love filled her gaze.

I sat in the empty chair next to her and she startled, her eyes widening.

"Oh, hi. I didn't expect you so soon." Her fingers fumbled with the stem of her glass and she hastily set it down, the drink sloshing. She glanced at me then looked away, shifting nervously. "I've never done this before."

"Done what?" I picked up the new bottle of wine and poured more into her glass, then took a sip.

It was plush, smooth velvet down my throat.

I took another sip, and tilted my head at the threesome going on in front of us. "Watched your husband have a threesome with two men?"

She chuckled humorously, taking the glass from me amicably and took a long swig, shaking her head. "No, he's been with other men since before we married." She stared at them as they adjusted positions, not paying any attention to us. "He wants me to participate this time but I've," she glanced at me, taking in a deep breath, "I've never been with another woman."

I smiled to reassure her. "So it was his idea?" I nodded at her husband, "and you agreed? Did he have to talk you into it?"

"I think he feels bad and he thinks this will make it better." A shoulder came up. Suddenly her eyes darted to me, panic in them. "It's not that you're not beautiful or anything..."

"It's okay," I took her hand, my need to comfort her overcoming any shyness between us.

Her eyes fell to my hand, my thumb stroking her skin. When she looked back up at me, there was an openness there, a vulnerability that hadn't been there before. She leaned forward, her eyes falling to my lips. "I'm willing to try it though..."

Knowing I had to gain her trust, I lifted my hand, pressing my thumb to her lower lip. Then I leaned in and kissed her, inwardly smirking at the thought that Coulter was watching.

Her lips were soft and sweet from the taste of her drink but, there was no chemistry between us. She stilled, not returning the kiss, so I pulled back to look into her eyes. She laughed, covering her mouth with her hand. "Sorry."

Smiling, I shook my head. "There's no reason to force it. We can just talk."

Her shoulders relaxed and she leaned back, newfound respect in her eyes. "Okay."

"So," I leaned back in my chair, taking another sip of her drink, then tilted my head towards her husband. He was wrapped in an embrace with the two men, taking turns kissing them. "Why do you put up with it?"

Her eyes moved to him, sadness filling them once more. She laughed humorlessly. "Most people would think that I'm doing it for the money or the prestige--"

"There's no judgement here," I cut in. "We all do things that, from an outsider's perspective, others might not understand."

She nodded. "I'm sure you might know that more than anyone."

She was referring to the fact that she thought I got paid to have sex with other people. I just nodded in response, not answering.

She smiled grimly. "I really love him, you know?" I nodded my head, gripping her hand in a comforting gesture. "I've known him since we were in high school. We were best friends. I saw how he struggled with his sexuality. He doesn't even want to be gay."

"That's why he hides it like this?"

A shoulder came up. "That, and people would never accept a gay senator. Not when we got married anyways, though the world is changing. But serving in Congress has always been his dream."

"I can understand that. Sometimes we just need hope and that's enough." I nodded. "And you? What about your happiness?"

"I am happy. He's my best friend. Of course, I wish things could be different," her eyes suddenly hardened, "but I learned a long time ago that we don't always get what we want."

I opened my mouth to agree, when suddenly the door to the room slammed open, startling us.

TEN

Coulter

My whole body tightened as I sat, trying to appear casual, watching as Aster walked, her gorgeous ass shaking, away from me. I'd let her off without telling me what happened in the hallway, *for now*, but that subject was going to come up again.

Because I was going to bring it up and demand she explain to me what the hell happened, and I didn't mean that asshole who clearly was pushing the boundaries.

I'd already pulled out my phone to text one of the bouncers to find him and toss him out of the club.

I watched carefully as Aster approached the guard, then pulled up the video streaming app the instant she was inside the room.

Even though we'd assured the Senator that the room was completely private, it was a bold faced lie. Our line of work was much easier if the law looked the other way. The fastest way to get a senator in your pocket was by threatening his carefully controlled reputation.

I'd come to learn that the more powerful the man, the easier they were to control. They all had their secrets. Our job was to find them out, then use them as pressure points.

I was also using this same strategy with Nicholi. So far, Massimo Vitale was happy to find Nicholi's weaknesses and Dante's connection with Massimo was strong enough that he would play ball with us.

The Italians were nothing if not loyal to family, something severely lacking in my own.

I watched as Aster approached the doctor. Watched as she sat next to her, flirting with her. I bit down on the jealousy threatening to erupt.

Aster wasn't mine. She was a means to an end, nothing more.

In fact, I'd sworn to hate her, even though following through with that was difficult.

After a few minutes of talking, Aster leaned in and kissed the doctor on the mouth. I straightened, my eyes wide, horror washing over me. *Was Aster going to actually seduce her?*

I jumped to my feet, pacing the club and watching the screen in my hands intently, ignoring the complaints that I was bumping into people.

All my attention was focused on Aster.

Did she like kissing the doctor?

The camera wasn't close enough to tell.

Did her pulse speed up? Was her face flushed? Her lips puffy?

Her fingers were wrapped around the doctor's wrist. Was it in elation and excitement? Desire?

I stopped pacing, running my hand through my hair.

Jesus. Fuck. Usually watching two women kiss was only an invitation to join. But this time, I wanted to smash everything around me. *Was I actually jealous?*

What was wrong with me?

I hated Rose's sister, the little hellion. *Didn't I?*

Shoving my cell in my pocket, I strode towards the room, pushing my hand out to hold off the bodyguard. This was a King club, and no one told us we couldn't enter a room.

I exploded into it, slamming the door backwards, not caring that the Senator was going to lose his shit.

The three men startled, their eyes snapping to me as I strode into the room.

"Get out," I roared, staring them down so it was clear that I was talking to them and not Aster and the doctor.

The two men were already dressing but the Senator yelled, "What the fuck is going on here?"

I gave him an icy glare. "Unless you want the world to know the real you, I'd get the hell out of this room, right now."

The two men brushed past me, still in a state of dressing but the Senator didn't move to leave. He just stared at me in all his naked, halfway-fucked glory.

"Out." I simmered. "You can take the same private entrance you arrived in."

"I won't forget this." He sneered, moving off the bed.

"I don't care," I bit back, knowing full well that I would have to make reparations later, especially if he won his bid for election. But I already had enough videos on him to blackmail him into doing what I wanted.

Anything after his first sexual tryst at our clubs was only him digging himself deeper into the King debt.

I was actually doing him a favor.

Glowering with anger, he began to dress. When he was done, he strode towards the back door, barking out. "Marie. Let's go."

She stood, uncertain on her feet and that drew my eyes to Aster.

She was simmering with anger in her seat.

Was she mad because I'd interrupted her little kissing session with the good doctor?

Ignoring the tightening in my chest, I glared back at the Senator. "Marie stays."

"But--" he demanded, his face reddening in anger.

I interrupted what was sure to be a tirade from a sexually frustrated, but powerful, man. I pulled out my phone, holding up my other hand to stop him. "I'll send her home in one of our private cars." I tapped out several text messages. "In fact, to make up for this interruption, I'll send both of these men to our privately owned suite at the Dignitary. They'll wait for you there," I paused my tapping to look at him, "if you wish to join them." I grinned. "This will all be on the house."

He didn't answer me, but his anger quickly subsided, replaced by a lust simmering in his gaze.

"Well?" I asked him impatiently.

He hesitated, his gaze moving from me to the doctor. "Marie?" He sounded genuine, as if asking for her permission, which surprised me.

"I don't know," she hemmed.

I turned to see Aster place her hand over Marie's, her voice soft. "Stay with us. Please."

Jealousy rolled in my gut but I clamped down on my emotions, remaining cold and emotionless.

I met Marie's eyes, demanding, "Stay."

"You don't have to," the Senator tried to interrupt me but I kept my back to him.

"She does." I kept my voice firm; there was no room for discussion, and I ignored the scathing look Aster shot me.

I would deal with her later.

"Marie," the Senator said again, except this time, it was more of a pleading.

She sighed, running her fingers over the top of the table.

Finally, she waved her hand at him. "Fine. You can go. I'll meet you at the house."

In a few strides, he passed me, grabbing her to give her a chaste kiss on the lips. I shot out another text, then put the phone away, satisfied.

Some men were so easy to manipulate. By the look on his face when he turned to leave, his thoughts were already on the rest of his night.

As soon as he was gone, Marie turned to me. "I'm only staying because you picked me up that day. It shows that you have some sense of decency, unlike your father."

I nodded. It was fine to let her think that she'd had a choice in the matter.

"Sit." I gestured to the chair, my voice polite but firm.

She grumbled as she sat, looking at Aster. "And you work for this guy?"

Aster didn't answer and I easily moved the plush, leather chair up to their table. "Now." I sat down, leaning back to look at them, my hands templed in front of me. "You're going to tell me what I need to know."

Marie huffed. "If you think that I'm more afraid of you than Nero, you have another thing coming."

My eyes flashed, my anger building. "You have no idea of what I'm capable of. You have somewhat of an idea of what Nero could do to you, but I'm the unknown in this equation and," I leaned forward to stare into her eyes, "therefore, that means that the sky is the limit."

She scowled, her lips tightening.

"Marie," Aster began, once again, her hand going to soothe over Marie's, and I bit down on the bark that wanted to leave my mouth that she remove her hand immediately, "he's only trying to help you."

"No, he's not. He's only trying to save his own skin." Marie's eyes were filled with a seething resentment. "That's all the Kings ever care about. Themselves."

"That's not true," Aster disagreed.

"And how do you know that?" Marie spit out.

"I know because Coulter is trying to save my sister." Aster's voice was soft. There was no doubt of the vulnerability in her tone. She was as genuine as I was cold.

Marie visibly softened. "What happened to your sister?"

"Nero is keeping her captive." I held my breath, waiting for Aster to give me away, that we were keeping *her* captive too. But it didn't come. "Coulter is only trying to help her, that's why he needs to know what Nero plans to do with Bourbon's blood."

"Wait," Marie straightened, "it's *your* sister that Bourbon is marrying?"

Aster nodded, and Marie frowned.

"When I saw them, she didn't look like she was being forced to marry Bourbon against her will. In fact, she looked very cozy on his arm."

"She isn't," I grit out, but Aster interrupted me again, rushing to reassure her, even though she hadn't seen it with her own eyes.

"She loves Bourbon, but she's still under Nero's thumb. Coulter is trying to free them from Nero. But he can't do that unless you tell him what you've done with Bourbon's blood."

Marie bit down on her lip, but her fingers tightened in Aster's hold. "Do you really believe that he," she nodded towards me, "can help your sister?"

To my astonishment, Aster didn't hesitate. "Yes," she leaned forward to fully capture Marie's gaze, "I have to believe it, to hope. Do you understand?"

Something unspoken passed between them that I didn't understand and Marie nodded. Then she inhaled a deep breath. "Yes, I understand." She looked up at me. "I will help you, but, I have one condition first."

I tried not to appear too eager, but I couldn't help the thrill that ran through me.

I'd been right to bring Aster into this.

She was a natural.

She'd managed to do something in only a few minutes that I hadn't been able to do in several days: gain the doctor's trust.

"Tell me," I demanded.

"Your father," Marie's eyes shifted to Aster, who nodded encouragingly. Marie took in a deep breath. "He took something from me. I need it back."

"What is it?" I growled.

"A notebook."

"A what?" I asked.

"It's a journal, my father's. It's very important. Somehow your father found out about it and managed to steal it."

"What's he asked for in return? What are you doing with the blood?"

"You mean, what *did* I do with the blood?"

My own blood turned to ice, and I growled out again, anxious now. "Tell me what you did with it."

She shook her head. "No, I need assurances first. I haven't given Nero my findings, yet. I'll be able to hold him off for only a few more days, but I need the notebook first. Then I'll tell you."

I stood up, clenching my teeth. "No. You'll tell me first, then I'll give you the notebook."

She jerked to her feet, facing me down. "This woman may trust you, but your father will kill me if he knows that I told you. I need assurances first that you can get me the notebook. Then we'll address my safety, before I give you the information."

"But your husband--"

"Is nothing if he went against your father, and we both know it."

Silence filled the air and we stared each other down in a lock of wills.

Understandably, she was truly afraid of my father. I could see it in the trembling of her lip and her fingers. The defensive posture with which she held herself.

And yet, I was in the same position.

I *needed* that information.

I didn't know why, but something told me that knowing what she was going to do with Bourbon's blood was vital to our safety.

"Marie," Aster slowly stood, turning Marie's attention back to her, "I give you my word. We will find the notebook and get it back to you. Then we'll get you to safety."

"There is no *we*," I gritted out through clenched teeth.

"Yes there is," Aster's gaze flashed to me, showing her determination. "I'm just as involved in this as you."

"No you aren't."

"Yes I am! Bourbon's your brother, just like Rose is my sister. I have just as much of a stake in this as you do." Her eyes narrowed. "In fact, I'd say I have more."

The threat was clear. If I didn't let her help, she'd reveal to Marie that she was just as much a captive as Rose. Then I'd lose Marie's trust.

I didn't give a flying fuck what she told Marie. I wasn't putting Aster in any danger.

"No."

"Yes."

Marie interrupted our stand off. "You say you can protect me. Prove it. She says she trusts you. Let her help. Keep her safe. Then it will prove that I can trust you."

"No." I was really grinding my teeth down now.

"Fine." Marie crossed her arms across her chest. "You've just shown me that I shouldn't trust you."

"Exactly," Aster crossed her own arms across her chest, the two were mirrors of each other, uniting in female solidarity.

I stared them down, wishing I could shoot actual daggers from my eyes.

"Fine," I grit out, only conceding because Bourbon and Rose's life was on the line too. "But you do exactly what I say, when I say it. No back talking or going off on your own."

"Of course." Aster bat her eyes at me, then gave me a devilish grin, like she'd known I would give in. "Don't I always?"

"Time to go." I gripped her arm, pulling her towards the door, *the bloody nightmare*. As we left, I threw over my shoulder towards Marie. "Carlos is waiting at the back door to take you home."

Then I dragged a smirking Aster from the room grumbling, "You have no idea how much trouble you've gotten yourself into."

ELEVEN

Aster

COULTER WAS SILENT THE WHOLE WAY BACK TO THE house, his fingers clenched tight on the steering wheel. He wouldn't look at me and was short if I attempted conversation.

Disappointment coiled in my stomach and chest. I thought he'd be proud of me. Instead, I got some strange version of him being pissed off—that I'd done what he'd asked of me.

I might not have gotten *exactly* what he wanted, but we were at least a step ahead. Marie was beginning to trust us and that was *because of me*, not his rude ass.

A thank you and maybe a cold beer with squeezed lime was in order, but apparently all I was getting was the cold shoulder.

As we approached the gate to Coulter's house, he barked at me to climb in the back. I considered refusing but I knew the fastest way to getting locked back up was to get caught.

I could only count my lucky stars that he didn't make me put that dumb bag on my face as he snuck me back into the house. As soon as we got to his room, I rounded in on him.

"What the hell Coulter? Why are you acting like I did something wrong?"

"You betrayed me in there."

My mouth dropped open. "I did no such thing."

"You did." He walked off, his fingers going to the tie at his throat.

I followed him into the closet. "I did exactly what you asked me to do."

"I asked you to get information from her, not gang up on me." He threw off his shoes and socks, then shrugged out of his coat with jerky movements, hanging it up.

"She did give us information. She told us about the note-book. She--"

"You forced my hand in there! Made it look like I wasn't in control!" He wrenched the tie from his neck, tossing it on the floor. "Of course she didn't think I could protect her. If I can't even keep you under control," his fingers went to the buttons of his shirt, flicking them open, "how am I supposed to prove to her that I can protect her from my own father?"

"I helped you, not hurt you in—"

He peeled off his shirt, revealing a broad, muscled chest and stomach. A gorgeous tattoo filled the right shoulder and spread down his arm. I opened my mouth again to speak but my brain short circuited, distracted by smooth skin interrupted by three stark scars on his chest.

"In..."

"In what, Aster?" His hands went to the button on his pants, and I shrieked, turning around as he unzipped his pants and stepped out of them.

Not because I was afraid of seeing him naked.

Because I was afraid of *my reaction* to seeing him without clothing on.

It's just a body, I chanted, squeezing my eyes shut. *It's just an almost naked body. You don't want to run your fingers over his skin. He's being an asshole, remember?*

"Explain to me, how you *helped* me?" his voice was a low growl. And it was way too close to me.

My breath hitched, and I scrambled to remember what I was trying to say.

I crossed my arms and stared out the doorway to the closet, pretending I couldn't feel him near my back. "Every woman judges a man by how they treat the women around them. You giving in to me made her trust you *more*, not less."

"You really think so, little nightmare?" His voice was right next to my ear. Taunting me.

"I know so."

Suddenly an arm wrapped around me, swirling me around and pushing me back into the wall behind me. He grabbed my chin, forcing me to look into his angry gaze. "You have no regard for your own safety. What if something happens to you? It's like you *want* to be like those women I showed you tonight."

"She wasn't going to tell you shit, not without my help." I stood my ground, my hands fisting at my side as I stared up at the looming giant over me. "You asked me to help, and I did. I even kissed her, for fucks sake."

"Yeah, I saw the kiss," he growled, stepping closer so I had to crane my neck to look up into his face. "Is that what this is really all about? You liked kissing her? So you inserted yourself into my business so you could see her again?"

"What the hell are you talking about? I'm trying to help you help Rose." My chest was heaving, I was so pissed. He'd put on sweatpants and tennis shoes, but he still didn't have on a t-shirt. I pressed my hands against his bare chest, pushing against it but he didn't budge. "I didn't even want to kiss her. I only did it because you told me to seduce her."

"You mean to tell me that it meant nothing to you?"

"No! Why would it?"

"Because, you two seemed incredibly cozy when I walked in there."

"That was because we were doing 'girl' bonding, just like you told me to do. She doesn't like women any more than I do; it was just something her husband wanted her to try out. Why the hell are you being such a prick anyways? I helped you in there."

"Because," his eyes darkened, like the coming of a storm. "Don't you see, Aster? It's staring you right in the face."

"See what? What the hell are you talking about?"

"God you're so blind!"

I bristled at his words. "And you're a prick. What else is new?"

"Because, Aster," he slammed a hand over my head, hitting the wall, "I wanted to be the one you kissed, not her."

I sucked in a breath, stunned, staring up at him in surprise, hating him and wanting him at the same time.

"Then why the hell haven't you?" I snarked, "I thought the *Kings* took—"

Cupping my cheeks, he jerked me forward, slamming his lips against mine.

I froze in complete and utter shock, then gave in to it as he claimed my mouth.

His fingers tightened, one hand moving to wrap around my back, cupping the nape of my neck. He let out a guttural moan, his kiss dominating and controlling as his fingers fisted my hair.

He kissed me like a man starving, his arm clutching me tight like he not only wanted to kiss me...

He wanted to *own* me.

Shit. What that did to me.

I grabbed his shoulders, pushing him back. We stared at each other, heaving. Then twisting, I shoved him against the wall. His head fell back, his eyes wide with shock. I jumped up and into his arms, kissing him. Growling, he grabbed my ass, jerking me tight against him. I folded my arms around his neck, heat flooding my system as we kissed.

His bare chest against my almost nakedness set flames licking my skin. I ached all over, the need for him consuming me.

Stepping forward, he slammed me back against the opposite wall, each of us fighting for dominance over the other. I mewled with want against his lips, my hips shifting, searching for the friction I needed so badly. I hated this jerk as much as I wanted to fuck him.

"Want you, baby nightmare." He groaned into my mouth, his hands roaming, sliding under velvet until he was kneading my ass. "Do you want me, too?"

I nodded against him.

"You touch yourself thinking about me, all alone in that big bed? Dream about me sliding up into you at night?"

"Yes," I breathed, my face red. *How did he know that?*

"It's okay," he chuckled. "I fuck my cock in the shower thinking about you."

"Oh god." I groaned against his lips at the admission.

"I want you on your knees, staring up at me with those goddamn beautiful emerald eyes. Your hands tied behind your back, your freckled tits pressed out on display." His hand slid over my stomach, tickling the skin there, "Want to lower you to the ground, watch your face as I eat you out, over and over, while you're helpless to stop me."

"Do it," I hissed.

"I need to teach you a lesson first." His hand, tangled in my hair, clenched tighter, his kissing growing more intense as he murmured against my lips. "Teach you how to behave yourself in front of others."

"I know how to behave. It's you who needs to learn."

"You think you can teach me, baby nightmare?"

"I know I can."

He chuckled, low and dark. "I would love to see you try."
His hand slid down to between my thighs, his fingers sliding
over the softness of the velvet material. "You're so fucking hot.
Like fire between those legs. Is this for me?"

"Yes," I exhaled, shifting my hips, needing, wanting.

"You wet, little nightmare? Wet for me?"

"God, yes."

"Show me, Aster. Show me how bad you want me."

I grabbed his hand and shoved it inside my bottoms,
maneuvering his fingers at my slit. Then I rocked against
him, practically begging him to slide them up inside me.
"Can you feel how wet I am for you? I want you to fuck me,
Coulter."

He froze, then pulled back. "Aster."

"What?" I hummed with want, shifting my hips again. I
leaned forward, ready to kiss him again, but he suddenly ripped
his hand from mine, jerking it backwards like he'd just been
burnt. Then he slammed me back against the wall again and
my lips parted in shock.

"No." His expression was ferocious, his gaze cooling.

"What?"

"No. We can't do this. Even if we want it."

"If?" His refusal burned, and he didn't answer me.

Unbelievable! I stared at him, my lust quickly dissolving
into anger. I dropped my legs, pushing him away to storm out of
the closet, grabbing my pajamas at the same time.

"Get out," I demanded, yanking down the zipper to the
boots.

"Aster." Coulter began, his voice low, but I ignored it,
throwing off my boots and fish net stockings.

"I said. Get. Out." I stripped off the top, then swiveled

towards him, waiting for him to leave before I finished undressing.

"Aster, you have to understand--"

"Oh, I understand, all right." I fumed. "Now get out."

His face hardened. "I'm going running. We'll talk about this tomorrow."

"There's no need."

"Fine." He walked towards the door. "But now you've gotten yourself involved. You'd better be ready to suffer the consequences. We start working on getting the notebook tomorrow."

"Fine by me!" I yelled.

"Fine by me, too," he said, slamming the door behind him.

I stared at the doorway, heaving in anger. I couldn't believe only moments ago I'd been so willing to fuck him.

Now all I could feel was the burn of his rejection.

I quickly changed into my pajamas and slid under the covers, once again squeezing my eyes tight, willing myself to sleep.

TWELVE

Aster

IT TOOK ME FOREVER TO FALL ASLEEP, MY ANGER WAS SO intense. I tossed and turned all night, filled with nightmares of drowning in the ocean. I was restless until I felt strong arms around me, a low, calming voice lulling me back to a dreamless sleep.

When I awoke, the bed next to me was empty, and I wondered if I'd dreamed about the mysterious prince of hell who soothed *nightmare* maidens back to sleep.

I spent the whole day by myself, not even bothering to try to get out of the room or contact him. If I was going to help him, he knew how to find me. Marisol brought me my food, as usual, but this time she stayed longer to talk to me.

By the middle of the day, I was growing restless, and spent several minutes staring outside of the window at the pool.

The view from Coulter's room was higher up than my first one, and had a much better view of the sparkling water. But what I really wanted was to get my hands on that garden.

I itched with need and decided, *screw it*. Humming a Britney Spears song, I bustled around the room, gathering what

I needed to make my escape. Even if I didn't make it far, at least I'd get some exercise in. And the garden was just too inviting.

Just as I'd started tying bedsheets together, the door unlocked then slammed back against the wall.

I didn't need to look up to know it was the bastard himself, Coulter.

I ignored him, continuing to tie two sheets together, singing out the words to *Womanizer* as loud as possible because well, it was fucking appropriate.

As soon as I paused to suck in a deep breath, I heard him grunt, "What in the hell are you doing?"

"Singing, duh." I answered, before belting out the lyrics as I worked on my homemade rope. The sheets weren't long enough but no matter, I had a shit ton of his button up shirts lying in a pile next to me.

After a minute, just as I was finishing up the song, he came to loom over me, a scowl on his face. "Obviously you know how to butcher an old—"

"And fitting," I interrupted.

"--song, but I'm talking about this." He pointed at the sheets.

"It's my new craft project." Grinning, I held it up for him to see, then fake pouted as his frown deepened. "You don't like it?"

"What's it for, Aster?" he grated out, his jaw flexing harshly.

I shrugged. "I need sun and air. If you're not going to give it to me, I'll find a way to get it myself."

He leaned over, picking up one of his shirts with a disbelief on his face. My fingers worked faster, double tying the material to make a bigger knot. I needed them big enough to use as little ledges to help me climb down.

"You *really* think that's going to work?"

I smiled to myself. Boys really needed to stop underestimating me. "Yep."

He had no idea the kinds of things I'd done as a kid, forever escaping my nannies to run free and wild on the large farm behind our house.

I was a wild child, and hadn't grown out of my need for openness and freedom.

Even though his presence loomed over me, I kept going, ignoring him. I was grateful that he was pretending that nothing had happened last night.

At least he didn't wave his rejection in my face.

I'd have burned his room down if he did. The idiot hadn't taken away my lighter.

He shifted and, to my surprise, sat next to me. "Show me how to do it, and I'll help you."

I yanked the shirt from his hands. "Or you could just let me walk down the stairs to the garden."

"But what's the fun in that?" He turned to face the window. "That's what you want? To see the garden."

"Yes." I flicked the buttons of his shirt open, then twisted it tight. "I've been stuck in this room for days, not even allowed to go to any other part of the house." At his protest, I added, "Except for last night, when you either wanted to intimidate me, or use me to get information."

When he didn't answer, I glanced at him.

He was still staring towards the window. His profile was regal, with a strong jawline and sharp nose. He had a new scrape on his cheek and a slight reddening tone to it, like someone who had a large ring on his finger had hit him.

I wanted to feel bad for him, but then I thought of how he'd kissed me last night, then rejected me like trash.

I could almost still feel him on my skin, even though I'd taken a very thorough shower.

The intensity of his emotions last night had burst from him like a coiled up snake, waiting to bite.

Then he did, striking my heart so harshly that I'd found it hard to breathe.

And now, his poison was bleeding through my body, running through my veins, sinking deep into my soul.

If I was his nightmare, then he was my grim reaper, come to lead my soul to its death with his tortured look.

Gritting my teeth and tamping down on my feelings for him, I tied the next shirt, wondering if he would even let me use my impromptu ladder.

Knowing my luck, one of the knots would probably come loose and I'd fall to my death.

At least it'd be quicker than falling for a cold man such as Coulter.

"What did you find out about the notebook?" I tried to fill the silence so my thoughts wouldn't stifle me.

He turned to me, his manner cold once more. "That's none of your business."

I crooked an eyebrow at him, undoing the buttons on another one of his shirts. "I think Marie would be severely disappointed to find out that you went back on your word."

"Marie will never know."

"Yes she will." I grinned, showing my teeth. "She's too scared of your father to trust you otherwise."

"I'm not putting you in danger," he scoffed, "you've seen what kind of sick tastes he has."

"I don't think you have a choice in the matter." Abandoning my project, I stood, straightening my spring dress. "It's your own fault. You made the decision to use me, now you have to deal with the consequences."

"Fine," he stood, his voice dripping with bitterness, "be

ready at ten p.m." His eyes drifted to my dress, "And wear something a little more subtle."

I crossed my hands over my chest. "What's wrong with what I'm wearing?"

"For starters, you need to put on a bra."

"Why? Too much temptation for you?"

"Yes." His responding stare into my eyes burned so hot, I had to look away. My skin prickled at his intensity.

Just like last night, it had come suddenly and unexpectedly.

The tension between us filled the air with thick sexual heat.

I wasn't even looking at him, instead, at the curtains blowing in the soft breeze, but his awareness on me felt like a caress across my skin.

I hated how attracted I was to him.

How much I'd thought about that kiss all night and day.

He'd protected me at the club last night, not only getting that guy off me, but comforting me when I was freaking out.

He brought me cookies and soothed my nightmares last night.

In every thing he did, he showed me that he cared.

And yet, his rejection couldn't have been more frigid.

And I hated how much it hurt, because I wanted more. Wanted the man who burned for me so strongly that it scorched straight through me.

My body was strung tight, my muscles tense, vibrating with the need for him to reach out and touch me.

Just one soft touch. A soothing caress.

Something to show me that this coldness was all an act.

But he didn't move.

I swallowed down the emotions threatening to emerge, willing them to go away. I wouldn't show him my true self.

Ever.

"What am I supposed to wear then?" I finally broke the tension between us, my own voice growing cold and emotionless.

"Jeans and a t-shirt. Tennis shoes."

His touch made me jump; I hadn't been expecting it. His finger traced over the swell of my breast, and I felt my nipples perk in response.

I didn't look at him, didn't want to see if his gaze had softened. I was afraid of the desire I may see there.

Because *even if*, and that was a big if, he did want me, I knew that Coulter would never give in to his feelings for me.

Men like him were too hardened and afraid to give in to their true feelings.

I *felt* his presence draw closer and I closed my eyes, trying to block out the largeness of his presence. The way that it pulled at me, bidden unwillingly, like gravity and the tide. "Please stop."

Ignoring me, he leaned down, his hand landing on my waist to squeeze it. He pressed his mouth to my ear, his breath over my skin making me shiver as he growled, "Wear something subtle. I don't want to gouge out the eyes of any man looking at you."

Then he was gone, leaving me to suck in a breath at the emotions tumbling through me.

THIRTEEN

Coulter

RECOVERING THE NOTEBOOK WASN'T GOING TO BE EASY, and I deeply regretted agreeing to let Aster help. She was a pain in my ass and one day, probably sooner than later, it was going to get us into trouble.

By the end of the day, I'd discovered which of my father's guards was with him when he met with the doctor.

Of course, I was taking a big risk by approaching his guard, but it was one I was willing to take. My father had too many hiding spots to search through them, and I had a limited time.

Since I had to wait until late to approach James, I sat in Bourbon's room, smoking one of Knight's old joints and worked, switching between my laptop and my phone, as necessary.

Since taking on Bourbon's old duties, I hadn't given up my old role managing the clubs, so I'd hired new people to take on some of my old duties. Our revenues in the clubs had also increased, though that was nothing compared to our other, shadier business.

The opening of Posh was a noose around my neck. The

biggest pain in my ass wasn't dealing with the fragrance company, but getting all the permits signed off. The county commissioner wanted a new vacation home in Lake Powell, and it was taking us a while to find one he approved of. I was tempted to find something to blackmail him with just to get the permits pushed through but, there was only so much Dante could do in a day.

I'd deal with it later.

However, watching Aster through the video had become an amusing part of my day. After I'd left the room, she'd finished her 'crafting' activities, then stopped to eat dinner and talk to Marisol.

I kept waiting for her to try to escape, but she didn't.

I became even more suspicious when she laid on my bed, not changing, but keeping on her lacy purple dress. She looked towards the window, instead of the clock, until long after the sun set.

When she slid to the edge of the bed and rose, smiling in amusement, I straightened. She was going to make her move. I studied my phone carefully, watching as she tied her makeshift ladder to the steady post of the bed, then she peered over the edge of the window, looking out for any guards.

I'd ordered them away, curious what she would do.

As soon as her cute little ass had disappeared out the bedroom window, I slowly made my way out of the room and down the stairs towards the back door, making sure not to alert any of the guards on duty.

Couldn't have them messing up my plans.

I stood in the darkness of the patio and leaned against the house, watching with amusement as she climbed her way carefully down the side of the house.

As soon as she was close enough to the ground, I silently crept forward, reaching her just in time as she jumped.

She yelped as I wrapped my arms around her and covered her mouth with my hand, stifling the noise. "Shhh, quiet little nightmare."

She sucked in a breath of surprise through my fingers, then her eyes narrowed at me. "You little prick."

I grinned, releasing my hand. "They call me the big prick, actually."

She grinned and it lit up her face. "You're terrible."

"Terribly sexy."

"Shut up," she scoffed but she was still smiling. "You're inconceivable."

My arms were still wrapped around her, and her hands were pressed into my chest, her fingers catching on the lapels of my suit. This close, I could study the pattern of freckles on her face, and I had the sudden urge to press my lips to them.

How would they taste?

Could I count them all?

The air grew thick between us as we were caught up in the moment.

She shook her head, breaking the spell. Then, grabbing my shoulders, she jumped up and wrapped her legs around my waist. The woman wasn't even wearing shoes, for fucks sake. Thrusting her hand upward, she whisper-yelled. "Now, take me to the garden."

Christ, she was amusing.

I decided to give her what she wanted. Maybe if I let her see the garden, she would behave when I took her out tonight.

I smirked, walking towards the backyard. "As you wish."

Her eyes widened in surprise. "You've watched the Princess Bride?"

I feigned confusion. "What's the Princess Bride?"

Playfully smacking my chest, she shook her head, "Dork." Then, smiling, she wrapped her arms around my neck, fitting so well against me as I easily carried her through the backyard, past the pool, and towards the garden.

"Farm boy, move faster."

"Mexican girl, I'll move as fast as I want."

"Prince Charming, time is of the essence. According to you, we have places to go."

"Little nightmare, if you don't shut your trap, I'm going to dump you into the pool."

"You'd like that too much."

"I said *you'd* be going in the pool, not me."

She blinked thick, gorgeous lashes at me, wiggling her sexy body against mine, reminding me just how much I *would* like that. "What if I can't swim? You'd need to jump in and save poor, old, helpless me," she leaned in, brushing her nose against mine, softly flicking her tongue across my skin that sent a bolt of sensation straight to my dick, "then I might find a way to subjugate you into giving me what I want."

"You wish," I grunted, my voice thick, "there's no way you could overpower me."

Brushing her cheek across mine, she whispered in my ear. "There's more than one way to subdue another person."

Great. My dick was hard now. "I'll be doing the dominating in this scenario."

"You wish," she said, grinning. Soft lips came down on the lobe of my ear, her teeth playfully nicking it. I didn't respond.

I hated this.

The way that I was falling for her.

How when I was watching her through the video feed, I didn't think about Lily or Rose or any other woman.

How my mind drifted to her when I should be busy working.

Instead, I found myself wondering what crazy thing she was up to.

She thought I'd forgotten about the lighter.

It was impossible, since every time I entered my room, it smelled of cigarettes.

As far as I could tell, she didn't smoke them, only lit them for a few minutes, then snuffed it out, filling the air in the room with its smell and nothing more. And yet, every time I was near her, just like now, there was an undertone of my body wash radiating from her skin, and I liked that.

Liked that she smelled like me.

She'd been the only woman to make that claim alone.

She hadn't been tainted by Bourbon's touch, and the primal urge to protect that rose in me.

We made it to the garden but I didn't let her down, only stared into her eyes, my hands clenching her tight. Her fingers snaked upwards into the back of my hair, a small smile curling the edges of her lips upward. She scrunched her nose, then bopped mine with it.

I felt the sudden urge to take away the sweet, innocent look she was giving me.

To mark her with my darkness.

To show her what it was like to be claimed by a Prince.

Not a King, but a King's son, one who could protect her for the rest of her life.

I'd meant to grant her her freedom as soon as possible, but it was becoming harder and harder every day to detach myself from her.

She studied my face, her eyes lowering to my lips and she leaned in, just slightly.

Once again, an invitation.

To touch.

To kiss.

To feel something, other than the cold hardness I was

growing accustomed to, even though I'd been a dick to her last night.

"Aster," I warned her, my voice low and dark. A promise that if she kissed me, she would live to regret it.

"Just one," she whispered, her tongue flicking out to trace across my lips. It tasted as sweet as the smell of the roses surrounding us. "Just one before that magic is gone."

Instead of kissing her, I fisted the back of her head, tugging on her hair so that her neck was arched backwards. "You won't want kisses from me, little girl. You're too sweet and innocent for this world."

"That's for me to decide," the words tore from her luscious lips.

"And yet, you have no idea how I will destroy you. Because all I will ever do is take and take, until you have nothing left to give." I fisted her hair tighter, and she whimpered.

Not in pain, but with desire.

I growled, the need to possess this woman overcoming me. "I'm giving you this one chance. Turn around and walk away. Go back to the room. That is the *only* way you'll be safe."

Her lips parted, an exhale of two words forming on them. "Fuck. You."

My gaze darkened. ""You want me to fuck you, Aster?" My voice was rough and demanding. I shifted my hips so she could feel my hard cock pressed against her stomach. "You only want *one* kiss? That's not possible, Aster, because if you open this doorway, I won't take one kiss. I will take everything."

Her chest heaved, her eyes wide and innocent, but her body still pressed against mine willingly.

Her hand slid upwards, her eyes defiant as she placed it against my chest, right over my pounding heart.

"I will take your kisses, Coulter, but I'm not so naive. There is no softness in that hard heart of yours. Yes, I want you to fuck me. To take me under this moonlit night, surrounded by beauty of this charming, rotten world. But know this, you won't take everything from me, because I will *never* give you my heart."

Anger flooded me at the reminder that I hadn't been able to capture either Rose or Lily's' heart either.

In swift, sudden movements, I turned her so that her back was to my chest, my arm still clamped around her waist tight. "Is that so, Aster?"

She nodded, heaving, her breath catching as I suckled the soft skin at her neck. "And what's to stop me from making you fall in love with me?"

"Me," she answered, but her voice was less determined than before. Her head was tilted to the side, inviting me to touch, to taste.

As I nipped and bit the sensitive flesh, I slid my fingers down to her backside, flipping her dress upward. I palmed her ass, kneading and squeezing. God, she felt so good.

My dick was as hard as granite, and it was pressed into the crack of her thong-clad ass.

Since she wasn't wearing a bra, I could see the tips of her nipples through the cloth of her dress. I lowered my lips to suckle the nape of her neck, and she moaned, reaching backwards to thread her fingers into my hair, pressing my face into her skin.

There was so little cloth between me and her drenched pussy.

I slipped my fingers under it, palming it. Her skin was smooth and clean, and I groaned into her ear, biting down on it harshly. "You shaved yourself for me?"

"No," she tried to deny it, but I could hear the falseness in her voice. "I like it bare down there."

"Lie," I whispered harshly, my finger parting wet lips to stroke against her slit. "You've already revealed how badly you want me." I found her clit, knowing the exact moment I touched it when she gasped. "You can't help yourself."

She clenched into my hair, encouraging me to keep kissing her as she rocked her hips against my fingers. I chuckled darkly, my tongue licking soft strokes against her luscious skin. With my free hand, I yanked the top of her dress down, exposing one of her breasts to the night air.

The nipple prickled as I played with it in tune to the flicking on her clit.

"Yes," she hissed, her chest thrusting forward into my palm, her eyes closed.

"Here's the garden you wanted to see so badly. Why?"

"Because," she gyrated against my hand, searching for her orgasm. "My mom and I used to garden together."

I smiled, pressing on her clit more harshly, knowing that she was about to come all over my fingers. Her hand clasped my wrist, urging me on, the other arm tight against my head. She was practically fucking my hand.

I played with her tight cunt, bringing her to the very edge of her orgasm until her whole body was strung tight, about to fall over.

"Open your eyes, Aster."

She didn't even think about it. She obeyed on command, opening her eyes.

"Now come for me, baby."

I flicked it one last time and her orgasm ripped through her. A soft moan left her lips, her stomach clenching, her cream flooding my fingers. I kept my finger pressed to her softness, rubbing her out until she whimpered, slumping back against me.

"Now you'll always think of me whenever you see a garden, and how I made you come exactly when I wanted you to." I pressed my lips to her ear, kissing her. "You *will* give your heart to me, Aster, I swear it. Then, as soon as you hand it over, I will crush it to a pulp."

FOURTEEN

Coulter

I made Aster change because I was serious about someone else looking at her. She was being defiant from what happened in the garden but I ignored her as we made our way to Escape, one of the lower class stripper joints my father owned and where we'd talk to James.

I could still smell her pussy on my fingers: I wished the smell would never go away.

"Since I'm taking you with me, you need to swear to do what I say, when I say it."

She gave me a feral grin, her voice mocking. "Yes, Daddy."

I liked the sound of that too much, but it was not the time for games. I frowned, snapping my fingers in her face. "Stop fucking around. Now is not the time to be smart. We have to focus or we could mess things up. Not only for us, but for Bourbon and Rose, too. You understand me?"

"Yes." All trace of sarcasm was gone, replaced by a seriousness that pleased me.

"We're going to meet up with the guard who was with my father when he met with the doctor. Now, I need—"

"Marie," she interrupted. "She has a name, you know. She's not just her profession."

"At least I didn't call her 'the senator's wife'."

She only exhaled, staring out the window, not answering me, and I continued, "We're going to question one of the guards in my father's inner circle. One whiff of what we're doing and we're in a shit ton of trouble. Understand?"

"Yes, sir."

Even though there was no snark to her tone, I reached out, clipping her chin with my fingers and forced her to look at me. "You will call me sir if and when I request it. Otherwise, Coulter is fine."

Her eyes simmered with repressed anger. "Yes, *Coulter.*" I let her go, focusing back on the road.

Not wanting to draw attention to ourselves, I parked in a public parking lot, instead of the club lot, then took the back entrance, using my key to get us through the door. Aster was quiet as she followed me past the manager's office and the dressing room where the strippers got ready. I didn't glance inside but I knew Dante was there now, in case we needed him.

Leading Aster down the row of private rooms, I stopped outside one of them to listen quietly. Inside I heard what I wanted to hear: James, fucking my spy, Brooke.

I entered, slamming the door back behind me and striding into the room. At the sight of me, James' eyes widened, and he scrambled to pull out and grab his weapon.

I moved quickly, grabbing his wrist and slammed it down on the chair, disarming him easily because he was so surprised. The gun clattered to the floor, and I went for his spare, grabbing it from his ankle, just as he went for it.

Tucking one into the back of my pants, I held the other loosely at my side. There was an awkward silence as we waited for Brooke to dress. She'd found her panties and was yanking them on over her stilettos. Then she grabbed her top, not bothering to put it on before she fled from the room where Dante was waiting to pay her.

"James," I faced him, made a tsking noise with my tongue. "I'm surprised. You're not usually one to break the rules."

"I didn't." He stammered, his deep-set, blue eyes apprehensive. His cock was still hanging out of his underwear, and his pants were around his calves.

Aster's eyes roamed the room, staring anywhere but at him and his now limp dick.

"That's not what it looked like to me." I grabbed the hem of his underwear, yanking it up over him to cover his privates so Aster didn't have to look at it.

"I swear," he stammered again, "I was only getting a taste. This is my first time, I swear it," he repeated himself.

My eyebrows furrowed. "You're not lying to me, are you?"

He shook his head, and sweat began to glimmer on his bald top. "N-no."

It was strange to see the beefy, tattooed man sweat. James was a well trained, faithful guard. Someone I would love to have at my back. But unfortunately, he was *too* loyal *to my father*, and his weaknesses too easy to exploit. Brooke was one of them.

"Because if you're lying to me, if you're not as loyal as I thought you were, then Nero wouldn't—"

"I'm not!" He squeaked out. "I swear, Coulter. You know me. You know I'm loyal."

He sounded genuinely fearful now, which was exactly where I wanted him to be. I stared him down, drawing out the moment, then leaned down to look directly into his eyes. "Then prove it."

"Anything."

"Tell me what my father did with the good doctor's notebook, and I'll believe you."

His eyes widened and his head violently jerked backwards in disbelief, confirming that he knew where it was. "You're crazy if you think I'm going to tell you that."

A cold calmness washed over me. I raised the gun and put it to his head. "Test me. See how crazy I am."

There was now true alarm in his eyes, but, as I stared him down, he hesitated. He'd known me for a long time, believed that I was much more willing to give him leniency than my father.

That was changing, but he didn't know that.

"Give me an out." Licking his lips, his eyes went to Aster, who was leaning over us, giving him her best menacing look. It was impressive. "I know you want to save her, otherwise she wouldn't be here."

I dug the gun in harsher. "Are you fucking threatening her? Because if you are, I will blow your brains out."

"No!" He threw his hands up in surrender. "That's not what I meant, I swear."

"You have three seconds to tell me where it is before you die, and Raven becomes an offering on the negotiating table with Nicholi."

I would never, *ever*, in my life, put his young sister in that position, but, by the panic in his eyes, he didn't know that. He was more afraid that I would hurt her than for his own life.

"Three, two..." I quickly begin the countdown.

"Fine," he growled, "but get that gun out of my head, and let me pull my pants up, for fucks sake."

I lowered the gun, keeping it by my side, and took a step backwards, giving him room to dress. While he was pulling up his pants, I tugged Aster into my side protectively, keeping her close. I was taking the chance that James would grab her and use her as leverage against me.

When he was done dressing, he faced me with more confidence. "You know Nero will kill me when he finds out. It's only a matter of time."

"You knew it was risky to work with him."

His face darkened. "That wasn't even my choice."

I crooked an arrogant smile at him. "Funny. It wasn't mine, either."

His scowl deepened as we stared each other down.

"Fine," he barked when he saw that I wasn't backing down, "but, like I said, I at least need a chance. Give me time to get Raven and myself out of here."

"You have three hours."

"That's not enough time!"

"That's not my problem."

Anger filled his voice. "Give me three days."

"No," I shook my head, "no way in hell. That's too much time. If we're caught, we're both dead."

"I'm not giving it up without time to leave. So I guess you have a choice to make, don't you?"

I snapped up the gun, pointing it to his face, ready to blow. I cocked it. "And I guess you've just made yours."

"We'll give you a day," Aster blurted out, and my jaw ticked. *Why the hell can't this woman just do as she's told?*

"No." I shook my head, but Aster stepped in between me and James, a pleading look on her face.

"Coulter. It's his *sister*."

I was sure she was thinking about her own sister, and the things she was not only willing to do for Rose, but was currently doing for her.

Just like I was doing for my own brother.

I grabbed Aster's arm, tugging her back towards me. She

should be grateful James didn't pull out a knife and use her to get to me.

"You have until tomorrow night to get out. Then I'm moving in, whether or not you're gone. Now tell me where it is."

His shoulders slumped in defeat, knowing he could be dealing out his own death sentence. "It's at his secret office. I'll give you the location and the code."

FIFTEEN

Coulter

WE APPROACHED THE WHITE, DILAPIDATED HOUSE READY to get in and out quickly. Aster was wearing black ripped jeans and a tank top, with her hair pulled back. The effect accentuated her beautiful, graceful shoulders, and brought out the softness of her freckles.

She was gorgeous, and I couldn't get my fucking mind off of her.

The gun strapped to her thigh only made me want to slam her against the SUV and fuck the shit out of her.

We'd spent the day shooting, and the sight of her confidence with her gun had me unable to stop touching her every moment possible.

Knight kept an eye on my father, looking out for any changes to his schedule, and Dante watched over James' activities. James had bought his sister a plane ticket to Houston, Texas, one she didn't get on, but instead stepped onto a bus, headed towards the east coast. One of Dante's men was on the same bus, keeping an eye on her.

James didn't leave town though, and last time Dante had reported in, he was approaching Brooke's apartment. She wouldn't leave the city with him, I was certain of that. I'd given him the time he'd asked for, and it was his choice to take that risk, instead of getting out.

The house was hidden outside of the city on a worn down, non-producing farm, surrounded by a chain link fence. It had a barn on the property that looked like it would fall over any minute, and a lone donkey munching on the sparse tuffs of grass.

My father had an important meeting tonight, and I had exactly thirty minutes when I knew he would be too occupied to take any calls coming in and out. Though it was uncomfortably close to our location, I was confident we could get in and out quick enough.

The night was quiet and the whiff of shit from the neighboring ranch tickled my nose. As I surveyed the back end of the property, my chest began to tighten. Something about this whole situation was off.

I'd never heard of this place before, though I was sure there was lots of things I didn't know about my father and his business. I reminded myself why we were doing this and led Aster towards the fence.

Marie said she could only hold my father off for a few days. If I didn't get the notebook tonight, she would bring the results, whatever they were for, to my father.

As we stood before the fence, I considered telling Aster to go back to the car to wait for me.

Scratch that. I would chain her to the fence. Knowing her, she'd fight against returning to the car.

She seemed to sense it though, and as she suddenly turned to me, a determined look on her face.

"We going in? Or you going to stand here like a limp dick?"

Christ. *This woman.*

I shook my head, pulling the cutters out of my bag and shaking my head. "You're a bit extra, you know."

She grinned. "You have no idea," as I began to cut the chain link fence, she leaned in to whisper into my ear, "how *extra* I can be."

My hands on the cutters froze.

Her breath washed over my neck. "Just try me, Coulter. You'll be an addict after the first hit."

My mouth was suddenly dry. My brain went blank as I imagined all the filthy things I wanted to do to this woman. She was right; I was already greedy to her kind of drug.

"Dummy, keep going." She punched my arm, snapping me out of my fantasies.

Growling, I cut through the fence quickly, then pushed it open, crawling through it first in case the security system went off.

When it didn't, I gestured her inside, and we both moved quickly through the shadows towards the side house.

One guard was stationed at the front gate, while another one patrolled around the property. I tried the back door—locked. I considered whether or not I had time to pick it before the guard made his way around this way when Aster grabbed my arm, pointing to a window.

Nodding, we moved quickly. It was unlocked, easily sliding open.

Frowning, I grabbed her hips and hefted her through it, quickly following behind her.

Once we were inside, I turned on the flashlight and took the lead, following James' instructions towards the stairs. The house was dark and sparsely furnished and we could only make out dark shapes in the light. The hardwood floors creaked with every step, which was really irritating and making me tense.

I kept thinking about that window. The sparse guards. How James went to see Brooke instead of leaving town with his sister.

When we reached the top of the stairs, I jerked to a stop and Aster ran into me from behind.

Swiveling, I grabbed her, yanking her from falling down the stairs. I pulled her into my arms, staring into her eyes. I pressed my hand to her mouth to stifle her protest. "Something's wrong," I whispered.

"What? Why?" She whispered against my hand. "Looks easy to me."

"That's the problem. It's *too* easy." My eyebrows furrowed as I tried to think. Normally, I would trust my instincts and leave immediately. They were rarely wrong. But there was a ticking clock over my head. We had to get the notebook tonight.

Suddenly my pocket buzzed and I let go of Aster, pulling my phone from it. There was a text from Dante.

Brooke left her apartment alone. Went inside, James wasn't there.

It vibrated again with another one.

Knight said Nero walked out of his meeting early.

I swore under my breath, then texted him back. *Get the hell over here.*

"You have to leave. Right now," I told Aster. She frowned, rebellion forming on her face, but I shook my head, cutting off her protest. "Remember? You promised."

"But--"

"Aster. I'm telling you to leave. Right now. Go back to the SUV. Wait for me. If I'm not there in twenty minutes, leave without me. You can go anywhere, run away if you want."

She clicked her tongue, rolling her eyes and whispered back. "I'm not leaving my sister."

"Fine." I didn't have time to argue with her. "If I don't return soon," I pressed my phone into her hand, "call Dante. He'll tell you what to do. The code to get into the phone is 5459. Can you remember that?"

For once in her fucking life, she didn't argue with me, but took the phone, nodding. Clutching it to her chest, she stepped up on her tiptoes and kissed my cheek. "Be careful."

"*You* be careful." Wrapping an arm around her back, I jerked her to me, kissing her.

She gasped and I cupped her jaw, tilting her head, loving the feel of her soft lips against mine. Her lips parted, and our tongues tangled. She tasted so sweet, so soft, so *soulful*.

I tasted *life* in her kiss, and I needed more.

I felt alive for the first time since I'd returned home.

She was right.

She was a fucking drug, and I was her addict.

I slowly pulled away, reluctantly, but the need to protect her overcame my need to taste her.

I nibbled softly on her lips, tugging them. "That's a promise for later."

She nodded. "Yes, please."

"Sir."

Her eyes heated. "Please, sir."

Fuuuck. I loved it. "Now go. Be careful. Scream if anything happens."

She nodded, and I watched her sexy ass as she turned away and snuck quietly down the stairs. I heard the soft creak of the back door. When I sensed that she was out of the house, I pulled out my gun, then made my way to the end of the hallway.

The door wasn't locked and I opened it slowly, my gun held out in front of me.

The room was empty, with only a mattress on the floor and a rolling chair, tucked under an empty table.

I moved quickly, striding to the closet where I found the false panel, just like James said. Typing in the code to the safe, I opened the door, and disappointment settled in my stomach like an anchor.

Empty.

Shit.

Fucking James. I was going to kill him when Dante found him.

I needed to get the hell out of here.

I made it to the hallway before the lights flickered at the window. Heart pounding, I raced into the front facing room, pushing boxes aside and tearing the curtains open to see guards racing through the yard towards the front door.

In the middle of them, was my father.

As if he had a second sense, he looked up, right into the window I was standing.

It was too dark to see his face but I thought I saw a smug, knowing look plastered on his face.

I didn't wait. I swiveled on my feet, racing towards the back room, planning on jumping from one of the windows, only to growl in frustration at the sight of the house surrounded by men. Stepping backwards, I scanned the rest of the landscape, searching for Aster.

My only comfort was that she seemed to have gotten away.

I made it down the stairs before the men rushed into the house, guns pulled out, all trained on me.

I dropped my gun, holding my hands up in surrender, waiting for the bastard of a father to enter.

James came in first and I growled, jumping towards him. "Asshole."

A wall of men swarmed between the two of us, holding me back. Someone kicked my legs, forcing me to my knees. Someone else jerked my arms behind my back, using a zip tie to tie them together.

James kept his distance, but his hard gaze met my furious one. He shook his head, scowling. "You threatened my sister, man."

I didn't respond, because just then, my father strode into the house. He was wearing his standard suit but without a tie, which was rare. The top buttons of his shirt were undone, and splatters of dark red colored his collar.

He met my gaze, his steely blue eyes so like Bourbon's, met mine.

It was the grin he gave me that made me freeze in place. Several guns were pointed at my head, and yet, strangely in this moment, I thought about Bourbon.

I wondered how often this had happened to him and understanding washed over me like a tidal wave.

While I was busy messing around with Lily, Bourbon had been at my father's side.

When we were younger, Bourbon had been full of life, and he'd mutinied against our father often. But, the older we grew, the colder and more detached Bourbon became, and the rebelliousness slowly drained from him.

I'd hated it at the time, but now, I finally got it.

You don't dwell with evil and it not touch you.

In that moment, any doubts about the kind of man I was becoming bled out of me, replaced with something stronger.

Something so powerful, that it would take my own father killing me to rip it out of me.

It was a fierce corruption of my own soul.

I had to become the devil to defeat evil.

I was going to do *whatever it took* to get Bourbon and Rose free, so they could live a happy life together.

They both deserved it.

And, as my father loomed over me, I matched his cold, manic grin with one of my own, and swore to make him *suffer* for his sins.

Tonight was going to be hell, but unless he killed me, I was going to outmaneuver him, no matter the cost.

SIXTEEN

Aster

I couldn't stop thinking about that kiss. The look in Coulter's eyes before his lips connected with mine.

The promise in his gaze when he pulled back. The flash of vulnerability, the *hope* in his eyes.

So, he wasn't an emotionless robot after all.

I was beginning to doubt he had it in him, especially after his words in the garden.

My musings fled as I waited at the back edge of the fence and a horde of headlights advanced down the long driveway, straight for the house.

I anxiously watched as they swarmed the house. When Coulter didn't come out after a few minutes, I knew something was wrong.

Creeping back through the large, fenced in area, I raced towards the old, leaning barn, searching inside it.

I swear I wasn't a pyromaniac, but if duty demanded it, I was happy to lend a hand.

I mean, they had exactly what I needed, almost feet from each other. It's like they were asking for it.

Happy to oblige, motherfuckers.

Dragging one of those wooden pallets, I shoved it under the gas tank of an old, paint-chipped Ford truck. The thing looked like it was from the eighties; it would burn nicely. As I poured a twenty gallon tank of gasoline on it, I wondered if it would blow up like it did in the American movies.

I wasn't going to stick around to find out.

Checking one last time to make sure that Coulter was still stuck inside, I pulled the lighter out of my pocket.

"You've been a good toy," I purred to it, then blew it a kiss goodbye, throwing it onto the bed of the truck.

I only waited a second to make sure it lit, then nearly burned my eyebrows off as it immediately caught.

I turned, sprinting back to the hole in the fence, grinning wickedly. It only took seconds to shove myself through the hole in the fence and the loud bang made me jump but I didn't look back to admire my handiwork. I had to get the hell out of here before I got caught.

I drove randomly for ten minutes, telling myself I wasn't getting myself lost, before pulling over. Punching in the security code on Coulter's phone, I scrolled through Coulter's contacts, easily finding Dante's number.

Tapping my foot and biting my nails nervously, I waited for him to answer. The shitload of trouble we could be in had sunk in, and I kept shoving away the image of the girl with the dead eyes from my memory.

"Coulter," a rough voice answered.

"Um, actually, it's me."

"Aster?"

I nodded, even though he couldn't see me. "I need your help."

"Where's Coulter?"

"I think they've got him."

Dante let out a string of curses, then finally, "I'm already on my way. Where are you?"

"I have no idea, can I send you a ping or something?"

"A ping? This isn't the movies, Aster."

"Idiot," I sighed, pulling the phone away to look at it. I pulled up Coulter's text messaging app, realizing that he didn't have any of them saved.

There went my plans to spy through his phone later.

I easily maneuvered through his phone, then put my phone back up to my ear. "There. You should be able to see me."

"Got it," he said. "I'll be there in ten. Don't go anywhere!" he growled before hanging up on me.

"Duh." I said to a dead line before sighing. I disappointingly found nothing of interest on Coulter's phone in the seven minutes it took Dante to reach me, biting my nails the whole time.

Another tinted Range Rover SUV pulled up next to me, and I grabbed the gun strapped on my thigh. When I saw Dante jump out, the SUV speeding off, I put it away, relieved.

"We need to get you back to the house." He jerked open the car door and began prodding me over the console.

"What about Coulter?"

"He'll be okay. I've got someone helping him." He pushed the gear into drive, then, tires squealing, sped down the highway. His dark eyebrows were furrowed but a small smile played on the corner of his lips. "I heard about what you did. You probably saved his life."

"Oh well, that," I waved him off, though I was secretly pleased. "It was entertaining."

"*Entertaining.*" He chuckled darkly. "I don't want to know what you would think is fun."

"Dancing. Singing to music at the top of my lungs. Throwing myself down a giant slide and off a cliff."

Pressing his lips into a thin line, he shook his head. "Just like your sister."

"Must be in the genes." We were flying down the road and I rolled down the window, sticking my head out to feel the rush of air on my face. After a moment, Dante grabbed my arm and pulled me back in the car. "Please don't kill yourself before I can get you back to Coulter. Because he *will* kill me."

"What? It's a good distraction. I'm worried about Coulter."

"When I say he'll be fine, he will. Okay?"

"If you say so." I nodded, not believing him. "What we need to do is find that notebook. They'll be busy for a while putting out the fire. Then they'll have to deal with the firemen and police. I wouldn't be surprised if Nero's hiding other stuff there. There's no way he'll take a chance and leave it up to someone else to take care of things."

Dante didn't answer right away, just stared at the road flying by as if it had personally offended him.

"I don't know about you, but I'm going to take advantage of the opportunity. And," I kept on eagerly, "two hands make faster work than one." I hoped I wouldn't have to physically fight him on this, because I was willing to throw down on this.

"Knight is already on his way to the house, making sure your ass doesn't get caught when we get there."

"You act like I'm the bad guy here."

"You insisted on working with Coulter. That not only puts yourself in danger, but Coulter, too."

"I--" I bit down on my snarky response, realizing that he was right. We were quiet the rest of the way to Coulter's house and I readily climbed into the back seat as we approached their gate.

The guard was a bit growley with Dante but Dante seemed to have some kind of authority around here because the guard waved us through. When we pulled around to the side, I prepared myself to argue my case once more, having thought of several good reasons on the way.

"Don't even--" Dante held his hand out, cutting off my beginning arguments, "If it were up to me, you'd have been sent back to Mexico by now. But," he grit out when I tried to protest, "for some reason, Coulter trusts your crazy ass, so I'm going to, too. *For now.*"

"Admit it. It's a good idea," I sassed.

"I'll do no such thing." He grabbed my arm, pulling me close to stare deep into my eyes. They were a dark brown, hardened and steely. In that moment, I knew I was staring into the eyes of a killer.

My throat was suddenly dry, filled with a stone lump.

"If you betray him, I don't care what Coulter wants, I *will* kill you."

"I believe you." I stared into his eyes as I said it. "But if you hurt me, I *will* punch you in your nuts so hard, your grandchildren will feel it."

We stared each other down, him with a vicious look on his face, me with a determined one. Then suddenly, he broke out into a grin. "I like you."

"Like I care..."

I petered off because he was already walking away. He lead me to the side door where Knight was waiting for us with a joint in between his lips. For the first time, I noticed that two of Knight's fingers were missing, and I wondered if that had anything to do with the three bullet-sized scars on Coulter's chest, or if it was common in the life of a Mafioso to have such severe injuries.

Dante grabbed the blunt, snuffing it out right outside the door. "You're going to give yourself away, numnuts."

Knight shook his head, grinning. "Nah, Wyatt smokes them every day, and he's usually out here this time of night."

"How'd you get him to leave his post?" Dante asked him.

"Let's just say, I gave him one of his favorite presents."

"Tatiana."

Knight nodded, the light overhead catching the gleam in his copper hair.

"Gross," I said to him.

His eyes finally fell on me, roaming over me in appraisal. "Nice to see you with clothes on." His teeth flashed in a grin. "Should we do something about that?"

Dante punched his shoulder. "Coulter will kill you and I won't do a thing to stop him."

"I don't need Coulter to defend me," I marched up to him but Dante grabbed my arm, pulling me away before I could do anything to permanently damage Knight's future children. "Come on, little she-devil."

Knight had done his job and the pathway through the halls of the large mansion were clear. We spent two hours meticulously going through Nero's office, moving slowly but thoroughly, making certain it looked the same as it had before.

The office had a black, marble desk and a black leather, straight back chair with a matching sofa across from it. Similar to Coulter's room, there were no personal photos. The guy was also a neat freak, every single thing had its place.

After going through it a zillion times, I slumped on the uncomfortable couch. "It's clearly not here. Where else could he be hiding it?"

They paused to think, and Dante's eyes moved to Knight. "You were the one assigned to watch over him. Where else would he have kept it?"

Knight dropped onto the couch, laying down with his head in my lap. "It's not like I watched him all the time. Just when he was with Coulter's mom. Only the ten minutes a week they spent fucking."

"When he what?!" I couldn't have heard him right.

Knight shrugged. "Coulter was worried about her."

"Oh, Dios," I sighed, rubbing my hand across my face, "you guys are disgusting."

"It's not like I *wanted* to do it. Take it up with Coulter."

No one mentioned the fact that he'd been right to be worried about her, since she was now dead.

"And Bourbon? Was he worried about her too?"

"They didn't have the same mom. The only woman who's been here for a long time is the cook. Probably longer than Bourbon."

"Mmm, I see." I put my hand on his head, running my fingers through his copper hair. "Where else would it be?" I asked, trying to think. If this were my dad's house, and if my dad was a psycho, where would I keep stuff to blackmail others?

Dante scowled down at Knight. "Get your fucking head off her lap, or I will snap your neck."

"You're just worried about Coulter." Knight smirked up at him, his brown eyes filled with mischief, but he sat up. "God you're such a pussy."

"No, I just want to keep my head attached to my neck—"

Their arguing became background noise as I tried to think. We had a barn out back of our property, but I didn't think the Kings had anything like that.

"Are there any other buildings on the property?" I asked.

Leaning back and spreading his arm across the sofa behind me, Knight took a piece of my hair and began to play with it. "There's the old maid's house, plus there's another one where the security stays overnight, but I'm not going in there. Too many of Nero's guards are in there. Plus, Nero wouldn't trust anyone enough to leave it there."

"What about his room? Or another room in the house."

"It would take us all night to search the whole house." Knight pulled the strand of hair through his lips. "He might not even have it here. There's probably a million other places it could be."

"Knight," Dante growled, "you must have a death wish. Quit touching her hair."

"Coulter isn't here, is he? So he'll never know, unless someone suddenly becomes a tattletell."

"I won't have to tell on you for Coulter to know. He'll just know."

"No he won't," Knight scoffed, dropping my hair. "You happy, you dick?" Then he turned away, not waiting for an answer. "Is anyone hungry?"

I suddenly sat up. "That's it!"

Dante reached forward, and, grabbing Knight's ankle, he yanked him off the couch, throwing him onto the floor.

Knight landed on his ass with an oomph, then growled and grabbed Dante's leg, jerking it. Dante fell on top of Knight, and they began to wrestle.

I stood up, sighing heavily and rolling my eyes. "Men."

I walked out the door, leaving them to ruin all the hard work we'd done trying to keep Nero's office neat and began to roam the hallways.

Within seconds, they were both marching by my side.

Dante, of course, spoke first. "Where do you think you're going?"

"I'm going to figure out where the notebook is."

"And how do you plan on doing that?"

"She's a girl, and girls have smarts," Knight said. "I'm sure she's got a plan."

"If she had a plan, she would've told us it from the start."

I ignored them as they continued to bicker, wandering the floor I was on, then headed towards the stairs.

Dante was right, it would take forever to find anything in a house this large. Fortunately for us, I had a better idea.

I walked down the stairs, and ambled around until I found the kitchen. The whole house was decorated with white marble, black framed masterpiece art on the walls, and bronze statues. It was all very sterile and impersonal.

The kitchen was a total contrast, the warmth in it almost at odds against the rest of the house. I could tell by the colorful back splash, intricately carved wooden cabinets, and the large, silver—and well used—stove, that Marisol had influenced the design of the place. I immediately knew I was on the right track.

Opening the refrigerator door, I began to pull stuff out. It was all random shit and had nothing to do with each other. Pickles, cheese, some green sauce, some red sauce...

"Mmm, I don't know what this is all for but I'm in." Knight was immediately by my side, except he opened the freezer and pulled out some ice cream. "Reeces. My favorite."

"I need something stronger to deal with you two." Dante grunted, opening a cabinet to pull out some whiskey. "Told you she didn't have a plan."

"Maybe she's keeping it a secret. Women like to..."

If they'd bothered to ask, I would've told them my plan, but, since they didn't, I kept my lips sealed. Ignoring them, I knocked around the kitchen as loudly as I could until, *finally*, Marisol came rambling in.

"Excuse me." Her eyes landed on me harshly, her hands on her hips. "How did you get out?" Then she took in Knight pulling a spoon out of the drawer, and Dante pouring his drink. Her throat bobbed, and she swallowed down the chastisement she was about to give me. "I see you're with Coulter's friends. That's okay then."

"Mmhmm," I just smiled at her, then began shoving every-thing back into the fridge.

Knight smiled, then walked over to Marisol, giving her a hug. "It's my favorite cook. Cómo estás?"

"Bien, bien," she nodded, biting down on her smile at Knight's compliment. Then she shook her finger at Knight. "You know I don't like it when you're in my kitchen."

Knight gave her a pouty look. "But I'm hungry."

"It's because you smoke too much pot. It makes you hungry," she pat his nonexistent belly, "going to make you fat."

He shook his head, "It won't, but your cooking will." He bat his eyes at hers. "How about making some flan for me? You know it's the best."

She sighed loudly. "Fine, but you stay out of my kitchen, you hear? I will cook it for you tomorrow, I don't have what I need tonight."

Sighing loudly, I closed the fridge door. "I've changed my mind. I'm not hungry after all." Opening the cupboard Dante was just in, I grabbed a bottle of tequila and waved it at Marisol, batting my own eyelashes. "I'm going back to my prison. Walk me there to make sure I don't run away?"

SEVENTEEN

Aster

THREE DAYS.

Three days of nothing.

No word from Dante or Knight.

Plus, there was a tension between Marisol and me, because, *I thought*, she figured out how I'd manipulated her. She hadn't even brought me any more cookies. And I was like, totally addicted to them, so I now considered her my medieval torture person.

Plus, three days of no effing sign of Coulter, and it was driving me mad.

Dante had assured me that Coulter would be okay, had seemed pretty damn sure about it, but how did I know I could trust him?

I went to bed the third night anxious, and I stared up at the ceiling for what felt like hours before I felt something on my back.

Fingers, brushing down my skin.

I jumped, my eyes bolting open, realizing that I'd fallen asleep.

I fell onto my back, my heart thumping loudly in my chest.

The face of Coulter loomed over me.

I squinted my eyes, trying to calm my erratic heartbeat, taking him in. He looked like they'd beat the shit out of him. He didn't have a shirt on, and you could see small round burn marks dotting his chest. Cigarette burns.

His stomach was full of bruises. Cuts, bruises, and indistinguishable marks trailed the rest of his body. Maybe they'd beat him with a whip? Or a belt?

The sight was sickening.

I gave him a forced smile. "You look like shit."

"I feel like it too."

His hair was wet, and drops of water rolled down his neck to drip on my face. He must have just showered. There was something else different about him, and it took me a moment to realize what it was.

His eyes.

There was no light in them. They were emotionless, cold, hard.

My chest grew heavy, aching for what he must have gone through.

I reached forward, tentatively touching his cheek. "Are you okay?"

He grinned, showing beautiful teeth and sensual lips, but it didn't reach his eyes. "I'm great."

My throat was suddenly dry, and I swallowed hard. "You're a terrible liar."

"I'm the best liar." When I didn't respond, his throat bobbed, his eyes softening. "You saved me."

My fingers moved to his lips, and I traced over them softly. I didn't want to talk about that. "Did you get the notebook?"

He chuckled humorlessly. "It's too late for that. The good doctor already spoke to my father."

"And?"

He shook his head, his expression darkening, and grunted. "Don't know."

His shoulders were strained as he leaned over me. I could feel his hands trembling from the pressure. The blackness under his eyes revealed how exhausted he must be.

"I may have something for you." I was staring at his lips because looking into his eyes made me feel so strange. Cold. Like I was staring into some kind of nothingness.

"You do?"

I nodded. "Yeah. I got Marisol drunk the other night."

He exhaled a chuckle. "You did?"

I pulled up a shoulder. "The woman needs more female companionship. She opened up."

He reached forward, shifting his weight to cup my cheek, while his thumb pressed down on my lip. "You're a little miracle worker."

I smirked. "I have some skills."

"What did she tell you?"

"Mostly she talked about you as a kid," I bit down on my smile, she'd had some interesting stuff to tell me about Coulter's mischievousness, "but she also told me, after she was really drunk, that," I lowered my voice, whispering for some reason, "Bourbon's mom was actually in love with your uncle."

Coulter stiffened over me.

"And that," I continued, "they were actually supposed to marry, but Nero took her instead. She also told me that it was a big secret that they'd continued on in an affair for several years behind Nero's back."

"Fuck," Coulter swore, lifting his head to stare at the wall behind me.

"Does that help you?"

He looked back down at me, and there was a strange shift

in his face. He slid his thumb in my mouth and, leaning down, he pressed into it, stroking my tongue with the pad. "Baby girl, you have no idea how much you've helped me."

Pulling his thumb out, he slid two fingers in my mouth. He stroked them, in and out, making my saliva pool and a flame crawl slowly down my skin to between my thighs.

"You've been such a good girl, little baby nightmare." He was pressed against me, his firm, strong body so heavy, just how I liked it. I was worried about his injuries but he didn't seem to mind. His gaze was heated, his eyes filled with lust. "And you know what happens to good girls."

His words made me ache. In my chest, my belly, down to the vee of my thighs. I wanted him to touch me there. To stroke me softly, to solidify the connection between us. I'd wanted him for so long, the need growing stronger every day. It had been torture to sleep next to him, to have him so close to me, and not touch him.

That needed to change.

I'd been a good girl, and I *deserved* my reward.

I didn't answer him, just stared into his eyes. Digging my elbows into the bed, I arched my back, pressing my breasts up against his chest and let out a soft moan.

His eyes darkened with lust, and he shoved another finger into my mouth. "Good girls get rewarded. Would you like to be rewarded, Aster?"

I nodded, choking out my answer around his fingers. "Yes."

His expression darkened. "Yes, what?"

"Yes, sir."

"Good girl." He slid four fingers into my mouth. "Four fingers. Four times I'm going to reward you tonight. Do you think you can handle that?"

"Oh God," I choked on his fingers, wetness pooling in my center. "Please."

Suddenly, he pulled his fingers out and sat back, his expression dark. "Take your clothes off."

I hurried to obey. It didn't take me long to strip off my silk nightgown and panties. He took the lace G-string and shoved it in the pocket of his sweats. "Lean back on your elbows."

I shifted, and did what he said. His eyes went to my breasts, heavy and needy for him. There was a fire in his eyes, and he lowered his gaze from my breasts to my stomach, then my legs. "Open for me."

I parted them, and the heat that radiated from his look sent a shiver up my whole body, making my nipples perk.

"Don't move."

Leaning forward, he parted my pussy lips, then leaned down and pressed a soft kiss to my clit. "You're flawless, Aster. You have the most perfect pussy I've ever seen."

I closed my eyes and leaned my head back, anticipation for his touch making my hips roll.

A sharp pain bit my inner thigh as he slapped it. "I told you not to move. Look at me, Aster."

My eyes flew open and I raised my head to stare at him.

"Look at me while I taste your pretty pussy." Gripping my thighs he yanked me down. Then, still staring into my eyes, he closed his mouth down over my cunt.

Dios mio. His mouth was so warm, and his tongue stroked up my slit, then pressed on my clit. My chest hitched, and the intensity between us heightened as he ate me out.

I'd never watched a guy do that before. Somehow, it made things so much more raw between us. More real.

My chest tightened, making my stomach clench as he lazily stroked, licked, and flicked my clit. I hitched a breath, whimpering. God, it felt so good, I could lie here all day and have him eat me out.

His eyes were molten, heated by lust, making me feel sexy

and wanted. They held me captive, not leaving mine as he brought me to the edge.

The fluttering pull of his mouth sent me soaring as the pressure between my legs pulsed, then detonated, shooting through my whole body like a thunderbolt.

I came, amazed at how quickly he brought me to my orgasm.

My heart pounded, my whole body shaking, as it washed over me.

"We're not done, baby," he grunted into me, pressing gentle kisses onto the top of my pelvis, then he dug his chin into my softness, the scruff of his jaw prickling my inner lips.

"My God." That felt so good.

He started all over, kissing and licking and flicking with his tongue, except this time, he pumped his fingers in and out of me.

He started out with one, then slowly added another one, and I felt so full. He added another one, stretching me, and I gripped the sheets, my head falling back, unable to stop myself.

"Squeeze your tits," he said as he slid his fingers in and out, fucking my cunt relentlessly.

I pressed my breasts together, and he groaned. Grabbing my leg, he shoved it upwards to splay me wider. "Next time, I'm going to fuck those."

"Yes," I breathed, feeling so exposed but so sexy at the same time. I played with my nipples, then pushed them together, giving him a show as my body tightened again.

He tilted his wrist down and his fingers inside me crooked. Pressing his tongue on my clit, he began to tap, tap, on something inside me.

Oh. My. God.

I came, screaming, my body violently shaking as my orgasm

ripped through me. I felt everything all at once, as if the sky opened up and poured lightning through my body.

I came and came, even as he didn't let up, until, exhausted, I pressed my legs together and turned onto my side.

He chuckled darkly against my skin. "Did you like that?"

I nodded, barely able to speak, a shiver crawling up my back as he trailed his mouth up my body. Kissing me softly, from outside my thigh, up the side of my stomach. Then he moved me onto my back, his lips tickling the skin of my breasts, his tongue and teeth flicking my nipples.

At the same time, the tips of his fingers brushed over my skin, stroking, caressing. So tender and sweet, like he cherished me.

His dick was thick and engorged, pressing into my thigh, my stomach, and I reached down under his sweatpants, wrapping my fingers around it. His eyes shuttered close, groaning, low and deep.

He leaned upwards to press his lips against my ear, kissing and nibbling, and I began to stroke him.

Somehow, his dick grew larger, thicker, and I whimpered, trying to pull him up and over me, desperate to feel him inside me. "Coulter."

"You want me, baby?" Coulter whispered in my ear. "Want my cock inside you?"

I moaned, nodding. "Yes, sir."

"Want me to fill up your sweet cunt with my seed?"

"I nodded. "Yes."

"Beg. Beg me baby, and I'll give you what you need."

"Please," I moaned, my hand moving faster, my body jerking as his own fingers went to my pussy, playing with it.

"Yes," I hissed, shifting my hips, fucking his hand as I pumped him faster and faster.

He groaned against my ear, a low, deep groveling noise that

had me gushing. "I'll let you come baby, but I need one thing from you first."

"Anything."

"Tell me what happened in the club."

I stilled, but he didn't let up, and I shuttered a breath, torn between his words and his fingers on my cunt.

"Tell me the truth, why you were so freaked out." He lowered his mouth to my pussy.

I closed my eyes, closing him off, not answering.

"Tell me, baby," his tongue rasped through my lips, "tell me and I'll let you come again."

"You said," I tried to speak, though my words came out breathless, "I'd already earned four orgasms."

"True," He nipped one of my pussy lips, pulling on it softly. Then his tongue snaked out, stroking over it. The man played with my cunt the way most men ate their food, like he was savoring the taste. "But I never said you wouldn't have to do anything else to earn them."

"You're such," I exhaled a breath as his tongue swiped over my clit, "a cheater."

"Tell me," he growled, his fingers crooking up inside me again, tap, tap, taping.

"Ahhh!" I clenched my fingers through his hair to make him press harder. I wanted to yeet him up and over me, then slide myself down on his big cock. "Coulter."

He stroked, filling me, playing with my clit until my whole body tensed.

Then he pulled out and climbed up my body, laying on top of me, his face inches from mine.

I whimpered, squirming, so fucking needy. This wasn't fair! I wrapped my legs around him, rocking my hips, trying to come again.

He chuckled, then, grabbing my cheeks, he kissed me. Slowly, his tongue thrusting in my mouth, exploring me.

"Tell me, baby. Tell me and I'll let you come." His fingers caressed my skin, so sweetly, but I didn't want sweet. I wanted to fucking come!

I growled, nipping at his mouth, and he pulled back, splaying a grin that finally reached his eyes. "You frustrated, little nightmare?"

"Yes." I nodded, then rolled my hips and clutched my tits, enticing him. His eyes roamed my body lazily, his hand reaching down. He slipped his fingers through my slit, stroking, stroking.

"Yes," I hissed, fucking relieved.

"You wanna come, baby?" He kissed me, playing with my cunt.

God, the man knew how to touch me.

"Yes, please."

"How badly do you want to come?"

"Please, sir." I skipped the step where he asked me to beg. "Please make me come."

"I just need a few words, and I'll let you." He pulled back and, jerking my legs open, he slapped my pussy.

I lurched, my eyes widening, my chest bucking outward as he stared down at me with those golden, predator eyes. He slapped it again then shoved his fingers up inside me, pumping so harshly that a vicious wave of arousal shot through me. "At least tell me why you don't want to tell me."

Tears sparked in my eyes, my emotions exploding under his touch.

I felt everything in that moment, all the experiences of my past shooting through my mind, my words bursting from me. "Panic attacks, okay? I get panic attacks."

Just as I said the words, the pressure between my legs shattered, and I came, screaming, tears draining down my cheeks at the same time. Pulling his fingers out, he pulled me close and tucked my body into his, his eyes filled with such concern. He pressed kisses to my cheeks, kissing away my tears. I wrapped my arms around him, tucking my head into the crook of his neck, the tears still flowing.

God, I hated feeling like this. Hated my angst, hating being vulnerable.

"Shhh," he soothed, "it's okay, Aster. You're safe with me."

He held me as I cried. Not big sobs, but I let my emotions go, draining down my cheeks in big, fat, salty tears as he comforted me, caressing me with his fingers.

For the first time in a long time, I felt safe.

Cared for.

My revelation hadn't sent him running, or closing off. Instead, he'd done what he was always doing: protecting and comforting me.

I squeezed my eyes shut, feeling like he'd built a shield around my heart. That he would take care of it.

I pulled in a deep breath, not knowing how I felt about that.

Coulter's life was complicated, and dangerous. And yet, I felt like I could trust him.

I pressed into him, needing more.

Even though I was asking a lot of him, I still needed more.

I took his hand and pressed it against my breast, being brave, and looked into his eyes. "You still owe me another orgasm."

While his gaze heated, and he trickled the tips of his fingers over my skin, making my nipples perk, he smiled. "Greedy little thing."

I nodded. "For you."

His thumb went to my lower lip, and he leaned in, kissing me softly. Then he pulled back and, rolling over, he stepped off the bed. He slipped off his sweatpants, languidly walking over to his dressers.

I studied his sexy body, the muscles of his back and perfect ass. The lithe way he moved.

"Condom?" I asked.

He shook his head, opening a drawer. "We're not going to need a condom."

My lips were suddenly dry. "Uh, what? Why not?"

When he turned back around, he had a grin on his face and a mischievous glint to his eyes. "Because, I said so."

He held out his hand, showing what looked like a silk tie and a bottle of lube. He had something else in his other hand, but he put his hand behind his back, hiding it from me as he walked back to the bed. Climbing on the bed, he quickly tucked the mysterious object under the sheets and out of sight.

Taking one of my hands he began to thread the silk tie around it. I let him tie both my hands over my head to the bed, and he settled in between my thighs.

Using one hand, he pressed them open again, and the cool air hit my pussy. He stared at it, running his finger through it, then pinching my nipples, alternating, making a heat pool in my belly again.

"Coulter," my voice was weak, needy. "Stop toying with me."

"But I like to play with you."

"I need you inside me. Now."

"I know baby." Leaning down, he kissed between my thighs gently, then suddenly, he ripped my thighs apart harshly, stretching them so far that they were shaking. "Do you trust me, Aster?"

I felt so exposed. So vulnerable.

And yet, I knew from deep within me that he needed me to

say yes. And, as I stared into those golden eyes, I realized the truth of it. I did trust him.

"Yes." I nodded. "Yes."

"That's good, little nightmare." His lips twisted upwards into a wicked smile that made me falter.

His finger trailed lower, then he shoved his fingers up inside me, slamming knuckles against my cunt, fucking me with them harshly, making it squeal.

Fuck. *Fuck!*

It was so fast, how he went from sweet to harsh, it made me so needy of the dominance of it. His other hand went to my throat, and he pounded up into my cunt with his hand, so rough that I was going to come any second. My head fell back and I bucked against his hand.

Suddenly stopping, he gripped my hips, then shoved my legs wider again. He flipped the top of the lube and squeezed it right over my ass.

Oh god. Not there.

"Yes there," he answered, as if he could read my mind. Then, without hesitation, he slid a finger up inside my asshole, lubing it up.

I sucked in a breath. Even though he'd used a generous amount of lube, it still burned. "It's okay, doll, I swear it only burns a little."

Leaning over, he began to stroke my clit with one finger, while inserting another finger into my ass. Then, scissoring, he began to stretch me.

It hurt but, with his finger stroking my clit, I began to relax.

His actions grew more intense, his fingers scissoring, stretching my asshole. I was so torn, and on the edge between pleasure and pain, with need strumming through me. I hitched a breath, the pressure building once more. Pulling his fingers out, he aligned his dick with my hole just as an orgasm detonated through me. Ripping me open as I was coming, he shoved himself inside me.

I screamed, fingers clawing at the bed as he moved, slowly but steadily up inside me to the hilt. He leaned down to slide his fingers up inside me. Pain turned to pleasure as his cock hit something inside me.

"You've been so good, baby, so good." He curled his fingers again, tapping, tapping, and I inhaled a breath, clenching my fingers into my palms, marking them with my nails. "But the thing is, I never punished you for being a bad girl that one day."

Suddenly, his hand was gone and my eyes flew open. I raised my head to look at him, and he revealed what he'd hidden from me earlier.

The top neck of the bottle of wine that I'd drunk, with the cork still intact.

He held it up to me. "You see, this was special to me. It doesn't matter why, only that you shouldn't have drunk it."

"What?" I tried to pull my hands down but they yanked at the restraints.

That damn wicked smile was back. Leaning upwards onto his knees, he adjusted himself. "Be a good girl, baby." Then, staring into my eyes, he slid the glass up inside me, cork first, and began to fill me with it.

Oh. God. What if that thing shattered inside me?

"So sexy. So perfect." He began to thrust, his dick in my ass, his hand moving the glass in and out of me.

My alarm about the glass intensified my emotions, and I clenched around it. Something deep inside me burned my own need into a fervor.

I felt a warmth hit my skin, and I realized it was his own blood. He was cutting himself with the edge of the glass. It only made me wetter, to see the heat and passion in his gaze quickly becoming lost in a haze of lust and need. He didn't care that he was hurting himself, his blood blending with our juices.

Instincts took over, and we fucked in a frenzy.

I was full of him in my ass, the glass in my cunt, and when he started playing with my clit again, I couldn't hold back any longer.

I moaned, deep and loud, so fucking needy and feeling so full.

"Yes!" I pleaded, moving with him, as he slammed into me, again and again, breaking me open, tearing me in two. Over and over, he pummeled into me, fucking my pussy with the glass then playing with my clit. My spine bowed, my stomach clenched.

"I'm coming!"

He ripped the glass from me, tossing it to the side and I shattered.

I came, fucking came the hardest I'd ever come in my life.

At the same time, he groaned, and his warm cum filled me up, sliding out of my ass as he pummeled me like a man possessed.

He bucked, one last time, then slowed down, still pumping, grinding into me.

I watched him, my chest heaving and the electric sensation of my orgasm washing through me. I loved, *loved* the fucking possessive look on his face as he stared down at his cum, leaking from me.

He smeared it on my thighs, the blood from his cut, mixing with it, his gaze burning.

Then he climbed up me, his sexy body humming and stretching as he untied me.

I wrapped my arms around him, loving the sticky, sweaty feel of his skin against mine.

We lay like that for a long moment, then he slid to my side

and tucked me into him. His fingers traced over my breasts, leaving smeared traces of cum and blood, and he pressed soft kisses against my cheek. "Are you okay?"

I nodded.

"Was that okay?" I turned to look at him and could see the guilt lining his eyes. "Was I too harsh?"

I cupped his cheek, and couldn't hold back my smile. "I loved it." Then I leaned up and kissed him.

He clasped my face and we kissed, slowly, softly, gently, for what felt like forever until my eyes blinked and I fell asleep in his arms.

EIGHTEEN

Coulter

"BRING HIM IN." I STRODE PAST KNIGHT AND DANTE AND into my office, and heard the scuffling as they dragged James kicking and yelling, behind them.

I'd never used my office for something like this before, but I may as well start now.

Leaning over, I gripped the edge of the rug and jerked it up and over, throwing it to the side. Didn't want to stain it, in case James thought his dick was bigger than mine.

As soon as Aster had fallen asleep, I'd cleaned both her and myself, then attended to my fucking wounds, and dressed in my blackest Bergdorf Goodman suit to match my mood. I was sore, exhausted, and in need of some serious pain killers.

However, time waited for no man. Aster's information came with a revelation, and serious action was required.

But first, I had to take care of this dipshit.

James fought against them but after several minutes of restraining him, and bolting the chair into the concrete floor, he finally stilled. His clothes were torn and drenched in sweat, his dark blue eyes blazing with anger, and dried blood crusted below his now broken nose. Knight and Dante dropped to the couch, with Knight leaning back, flicking his lighter with a lazy look. Dante sat on the edge, ready to jump to his feet for any reason.

I stood over James, feeling almost nothing. This piece of shit deserved everything he got. Hours ago, the roles had been reversed, and I'd been the one tied to the chair.

I pulled out my gun and, stepping forward, grabbed his sweat-slicked, bald head and jerked it up to force him to look me in the eyes. I pressed the gun in the middle of his throat and took off the safety.

His throat bobbed with fear, but he stared up at me with contempt and rage.

I leaned down, the smell of his sweat filling my nose. "The only reason you're alive right now is because Aster is safe, sleeping in my bed." I tilted my head to the side, shifting the gun. "Why didn't you give her up?"

"I don't owe you jack shit."

I ran the gun up his neck and chin, then shoved it into his mouth. "I think you do."

He stared into my eyes, defiance in his gaze, his words barely comprehensible around the gun in his mouth. "I'm not afraid. I signed my life away the day your father showed up on my doorstep."

"Is that so?" I grinned. "Knight."

At my command, Knight stood and went to the door. I stepped back, pulling the gun out and tucking it away.

When he returned, Knight brought with him a young girl of about fourteen. She had straight, jet black hair and bright blue eyes. Knight made her laugh and she blushed, clasping her hand to her mouth.

James' eyes widened at the sight of his sister. "Shit."

At his curse, she looked away from Knight, then froze at the sight of him.

"James, what happened?" She ran to him, falling to her knees on the cold concrete floor beside him. She was skinny, too skinny, and had holes in her knees and shoes. She reminded me of myself before I came to live with my father. "You're hurt."

"Raven," he let out a tortured sound, leaning his head against hers. "It's going to be okay."

"Is it, James?" I stared at them impassively.

Tears began to fall down her face and she swirled towards me, angry. "What did you do to him?" She turned her gaze to Knight, betrayal in her expression. "You did this."

I stepped forward and squat down in front of her. "Sweetheart," I gave her a comforting smile, "James did this to himself."

"Liar!" She was practically spitting fire, her blue eyes blazing. Apparently, their fiery personality was genetic.

I shook my head. "I'm not." I loosened my tie, then began to undo the top buttons of my shirt.

"Coulter," Dante growled, but I ignored him.

Reaching forward, I took Raven's hand, and, pulling my shirt apart so she could see the wounds on my chest, I led her hand to them.

"See this, Raven? James did this to me."

At the first touch on my chest, she yanked her hand back, like it'd scalded her. I didn't force her to look or touch but, at my encouraging nod, she tentatively reached forward again and softly ran her fingers over the wounds on my chest. Her eyes were wary as she looked at me. "He did this to you?"

I nodded.

She frowned, a snark to her tone. "Did you deserve it?"

I chuckled. "Probably." I stood up, fixing my shirt and tie. "Knight."

Knight stood and, wrapping his fingers around Raven's arm, he pulled her towards the door, despite her loud protest. The last sound we heard before the door closed was Knight reassuring her that her brother would be okay.

"Now," I said, standing between James and his line of sight to the door, where he was still staring, "you'll determine what happens to her next."

This time, when James looked at me, there was no defiance, no anger, only pure and utter defeat. "You win."

"I don't want to win, James, I want information."

"What do you want to know?"

"Why didn't you tell my father that Aster was with me?"

"Because she stepped in between me and the gun you were pointing at my head."

I shook my head, wondering how on earth meddling, spirited Aster could gain his loyalty so quickly.

She was impulsive and reckless. Yet, she still managed to quickly worm her way into people's hearts.

Even cold, dead, mafioso hearts.

"Tell me where the notebook is." I didn't need it anymore. I knew why my father had taken Bourbon's blood but, if my father had gone to the trouble of getting that notebook, it must be worth something.

"It's in his room, at your house, in the safe under the floor in his closet. The code to get in is 8405690."

"What's in the notebook?"

A beefy shoulder came up. "I don't know."

I believed him. If it was that valuable, my father wouldn't trust anyone with the information inside it.

I was done with James, except for one more thing. I stepped forward and pressed the nuzzle of the gun to his forehead.

He stared straight into my eyes with zero fear. It was admirable, the way he stared down death. "I have one favor to ask. Take care of Raven. Please. Don't let her get dragged into this world. She doesn't have anyone else."

I hesitated, my finger on the trigger.

"Please, Coulter. I'm begging you. If you want, I'll get down on my knees and beg."

I pressed the gun in deeper, leaning over to stare into his eyes. "I don't want your fucking begging."

"Then what do you want? I'll give you anything."

"Anything?"

"Yes," his voice caught, and I could hear the trickle of hope in it that wasn't there before, "whatever you want, in exchange for her safety."

"What I want," I paused, "is your loyalty."

He blinked in surprise, not speaking for a moment. "What?"

"You're one of the best guards my father has. I want you to switch sides." I was taking a huge risk telling him this, but I'd decided it was worth it. Especially since James now knew that I had access to Raven. "I'm going to take my father down, and I want you at my back when I do it."

His chest moved up and down as he breathed heavily, considering what this meant. Blood would run in the streets, but he had nothing to lose now. "I want to get Raven to safety, then I will fight for you."

"I will get Raven to safety. Consider it my gift to you. You'll know exactly where she is as soon as she lands, and will have access to speak to her."

James nodded, "Fine."

"Swear it."

"I swear my loyalty to you, Coulter, from here on out."

I slid the gun down to between his eyes, a dark look on my face. "Know this, James. If you *ever* betray me again, there will be no woman that will get between you and the end of my gun."

His throat bobbed, and he nodded. I let it sit for a second, then pulled it back. James exhaled a deep breath, slumping, and I tucked the gun away and stepped back.

"Dante, let Knight know what we've agreed to, and get someone in here to help James out."

Dante tapped on his phone, then stood to untie James while I went to my desk, sitting down. As soon as James was gone, Dante sat on the sofa across from my desk, his sharp, brown eyes on me. "Do you think he'll be loyal?"

"Yes." I opened my laptop, turning it on with my fingerprint then pulling up the secure website I needed.

"And if he isn't?" Dante cleared his throat. "Will you sell the girl?"

My eyes flicked upwards, "Christ, Dante."

He didn't react, only nodded. "Understood."

"Just make sure she's safe."

"Already taken care of."

"Good," I looked back down at my computer. "When am I going to speak to your cousin? The only reason I'm still alive is because I promised my father Massimo would be at the wedding."

"He's arriving tomorrow evening."

"Good, because plans have changed. Will he be open to that?"

"As long as you give him what he wants, he'll be open to any changes."

I peered over my computer. "He wants to be at the opening of Posh?"

Dante nodded. "He wants a private audience with Caspia Ferrari."

I furrowed my eyebrows. "Who's that?"

"She's the new face of Salvation, the new fragrance that's launching. He wants a private room with access for him only. No cameras. Back door access."

"Does he plan to hurt her?"

"No, but we can stipulate that the guard has access to the

room. If she screams, he'll hear her."

I sighed. "Do you trust him?"

"No, but I don't think he'll do anything to her. In fact, I think he might be in love with the girl. I've never seen him go to such great lengths to see a woman."

I sighed. "What we do for women, that's why we hate them so much."

"True." Dante chuckled darkly, shaking his head, and I knew he was thinking about the woman who haunted his own past. "Will this be a problem?"

"The fragrance company will have my ass if they find out that I kidnapped their spokeswoman and put her in a room with a mafia boss from Italy."

"She's actually mafia."

My eyebrows shot upward. "From where?"

"Ferrari?"

"Shit," I cursed, just now recognizing the name. "That could start things with Atlanta."

"How badly do you need this from him?"

I scowled. "Good point. Okay, let me know when and where to meet him."

"You got it."

"Now," I clicked on the video feed that I needed. "When I got home, my uncle Daimon was already gone. Do you know when they took him?"

"No." Dante sounded as if he was disappointed he didn't have the answer.

"It's fine." I began scrolling through the videos, though I wasn't certain this was going to be any help. "Regardless of when they took him, I needed to find him. See if he's alive or dead. The answer to that will determine how we take my father down. What have your men discovered?"

"There are three locations where they could've taken him, if he's still alive. Two of them are warehouses where he likes to keep his 'prisoners of war' as he likes to call them. One is a more private location." He cleared his throat uncomfortably. "It's your old house."

Eyebrows furrowing, I looked up from scanning the video feed. "My old house?"

He nodded. "Where you grew up. Before your mom moved in with Nero."

"Fuck," I whispered, my eyes back on the screen. It didn't take me long to find what I was looking for, and I checked the time stamp.

My father's guards took Uncle Daimon away at the same time we'd left to go to that house.

So, he'd known from the beginning that I would be there that night.

Fucking James.

I stood, slamming the laptop shut. "Come on."

Dante jumped to his feet. "Where are we going?"

"If I know my father, he'll have taken Daimon to my old house. If not, we have three days to find him."

It was three days until the wedding, when Bourbon and Rose should've had the best day of their lives. Instead, it would be dominated and controlled every step of the way by my father.

We were quiet on the way over, and I was glad that Dante had driven. I hadn't seen my old house in years; it wasn't a place I wanted to visit.

As we pulled up to the old brown house, memories assaulted me.

It was where I'd gotten burnt on the stove teaching myself how to cook hot dogs. Where I fed an old scraggly street dog named Max. Where men came and left for mom's work.

It was the place where, for the first time, I'd seen a woman give a man a blow job.

I was supposed to stay in my room but I couldn't help peeking sometimes.

Then the night there was a knock on my bedroom door, after I'd been instructed to go to bed.

It was Nero, and my mom explained that he was my dad. He'd loomed over me, a scowl on his face when I hadn't answered, instead scuffing my shoe on the floor.

"You hard of hearing, son?" His voice, cold and harsh.

I shook my head, my own voice a small squeak compared to his. "No."

"Then look me in the eyes when I speak to you. If you're going to be my son, you need to look someone in the eyes when they speak to you. That tells them that you're not afraid of them."

I shut down the memory as Dante and I stepped out of the car, shutting the door.

The night was *not* quiet, as Naked City came alive when it grew dark. But, just like it had only a few nights ago, my instincts warned me that something was wrong.

This time, I didn't hesitate. I knew what was coming. I just needed to verify it with my own eyes.

I strode toward the front door with no reluctance, and tried the door knob.

It wasn't locked.

As if something was waiting for us.

I flipped the light switch but no light flickered, so Dante and I stepped inside, our guns drawn, using the flashlight we'd brought to light the way.

The Las Vegas heat was sweltering this time of year, and sweat ran down the side of my face. I wiped it as we took in the room. The living room was the same, with cheap sixties carpet, peeling linoleum in the kitchen, and the same burn spot on the wall behind the stove.

A stench in the air filled my nose, and Dante and I met each other's eyes.

I nodded, and we made our way past the empty rooms and down the short hallway, opening doors as we went. Dante went into my mother's room but I approached my room. The same doorway where I'd met my father for the first time.

The door was partially opened and my chest constricted as I tapped it.

It slowly creaked open, and the stench washed over me like a wave.

I took a step inside, resolute to finish this.

I inhaled deeply, taking in every detail in the room. I wanted to remember it for the rest of my life, from the smell, to the sounds, to the way it looked.

In the middle of the floor lay the dead body of my uncle, his head missing.

On the ground, written in blood over his corpse, was written one word: *traitor*.

It was a warning, for me.

Betray Nero, and you die.

NINETEEN

Aster

I woke up the next morning to a cold and empty bed.

I frowned. So, it was going to be like that, was it?

I threw off the covers, disappointment coiling in my chest and throat. When my feet hit the floor, I noticed a small box on it by the bed. Curious, I squat down and opened it to find lavender smelling sitz bath supplies, and a box of freshly plucked rose petals with a note on instructions for a bath. There was also a small box of Marisol's cookies. Smiling, I grabbed one and bit into it, taking the box with me to the bathroom.

I spent all day switching from being annoyed that Coulter hadn't showed up, to reliving one of the best nights of sex of my life. Four fucking orgasms in one night. Most men didn't even know how to give one.

Later that night, after the sun had set, I heard the lock jingle. I ran towards it, a grin splitting my face.

I bent to leap through the air, planning on jumping on Coulter but, when the door opened, it revealed not Coulter, but Dante.

I stuttered to a stop, glad I hadn't pounced yet. "Oh, it's you."

He was dressed in a bespoke suit, with a gold tie and a brush of lipstick on his cheek. Yes," he deadpanned. "It's me."

I wiped at his cheek, rubbing the lipstick off, and looked over his shoulder. "Where's Coulter?"

"Not here."

"Wow, you're smart."

He grinned. "I know, right?" Without another word, he turned around, leaving the door open.

I stared at it in shock for a moment, then, not waiting for an invitation, grabbed my shoes, and ran after him.

The hallways were empty, the house still and quiet. Instead of going out the side door like usual, Dante led me to the front door, where there was a sexy matte black McLaren, with a soft gold trim and windows tinted so dark, you couldn't see inside.

"This your car?"

Not answering, he opened the passenger door, then turned towards me and just stared at me, saying nothing.

"Oh, you'd like me to get inside? How nice of you to offer." I stepped towards it, then hesitated. "Where are we going?"

He frowned. "Get in the car, Aster."

"Does Coulter know you're doing this?" I suddenly felt the need to question his intentions. The house was too quiet, and where were the guards that usually patrolled the front door? Everything was so perfectly laid out. Too perfectly laid out.

"Just trust me."

"Where are the guards, Dante? Did you kill them?"

He raised an eyebrow. "And if I had, would that bother you?"

"Maybe. Depends on why you did it."

"Just get in."

"I don't think so." I turned around to go back to my room, and Dante sighed, cursing.

"Here, Aster."

I paused, turning around to see what he would do. He put his phone to his ear, growling.

"Sorry to interrupt but she won't get in the car."

I heard the sound of Coulter's low chuckle and I strode to Dante, grabbing the phone from his hands to yell into it. "Where the hell are you, Coulter? You fuck me then disappear?" Dante suddenly became really interested in the tires, "I haven't seen you all day. I thought you were a real man, but apparently you're not, because real men stick around the morning after. They don't run from their emotions. No, a man like you actually begins to feel something for someone, and," I gasped dramatically, "oh my gosh, we can't have that, can we? Is that how you want to play this, Coulter? Really? God, you're so immature."

I took a deep breath, ready to keep going when Coulter interrupted what was probably going to be the longest rant of my life.

"I sent Dante to take you to see Rose, but if you'd rather stay at the house, I'm sure Dante has other things he could be doing."

All of the anger fled me, immediately replaced with a gushing of emotion. I clutched the phone to me, turning away from Dante and lowering my voice. "If this is a trick to get me in the car, I will--"

"No trick, Aster. Now just go. I'm busy."

"Thank you Coulter," I gushed with so much emotion, I was going to start crying. "You're going to get the best blow job of your life for this."

I was about to hang up but Coulter stopped me. "Aster, you're not letting your heart get involved, are you?"

I inhaled a breath, scowling, "I'm not the only one, buddy," then I *did* hang up and strode back to Dante, my head held high. "I think I will get in the car."

I slid inside while Dante chuckled, shaking his head as he closed the door with a smirk.

"Shut up, Dante."

He laughed louder as he walked around the door.

"I don't want to hear it," I said as he got inside, and he just put the car in drive.

The man at the gate didn't even look up as we drove through it, and it felt nice for once to not have to hide in the back.

I was jittery the whole way there, and by the time Dante brought me through the back door of a high end boutique, I was about to burst.

As soon as I walked through the short hallway and into a large grey room I heard a squeal.

Rose was standing on a platform, wearing a gorgeous cream wedding dress, and an elderly lady was kneeling at her feet, pinning the edges of it.

"Aster!" Rose jumped off the platform, ignoring the scowl of the elderly lady as she ran towards me.

Something loosened inside me. All of the fear and angst and anger I'd been feeling for the past few weeks bled away. And, as I ran towards her, a grin broke from my face and tears streamed down my face.

We collided in a mass of tears and laughing and squealing.

"You're finally here!"

"*You're* finally here!" I had my arms wrapped around her so tight, there were pins poking into my skin but I didn't care. I would let someone stick me with a thousand needles to touch my sister again.

The silver-haired lady who'd been pinning the dress

walked out of the room, grumbling and shaking her head but I ignored her. I was with my sister!

Rose pulled back, cupping my face. "You're all grown up."

"So are you."

We were grinning like fools.

"I never thought I would see you again." Her eyes clouded over, "not after Lily, and then my dad sold me to Dimitri and I thought that was it for me."

"That bastard!" Indignation filled me. "I'm going to kill him for doing that."

She laughed, shaking her head and glancing to the side. It was only then that I saw Knight standing at the edge of the room, watching us. "I don't think we'll have to worry about him any longer."

I straightened, my eyes widening. "Rose, did you kill him?"

She laughed, "God no, do you think I would do that?"

I shook my head, sighing. "Honestly? I don't know what to expect anymore."

She took my hand, leading me to sit on a lavender colored velvet sofa. "I know what you mean. And I'm sorry I got you involved in all this." More tears began to drain down her face, and I could *feel* the infusion of guilt coming off her. At this, Knight made his way towards us, a deep scowl on his face.

"Aster, did you make her cry?" He sounded...*not* like himself. Protective, of Rose, like he was going to drag me out of here if I told him yes.

"I'm okay, Knight. She didn't do anything," Rose waved him off, but he grabbed a box of tissues lying on a side table and brought it to her, giving me a dirty look.

"I didn't do anything." Scowling, I shot him the bird. Rose laughed, grabbing my hands and pulling them to her chest.

"You always were a firecracker."

I ignored Knight, who was still hovering over her protectively.

"Tell me," I gripped her hands tight. "Are they forcing you to marry Coulter's brother?" I gave Knight a significant look. "Or are you really in love with someone else?"

"Oh my god, no," Rose shook her head, "Knight is just protective, that's all." Her face turned serious, "He helped me when I had no one else."

"You always had Bourbon," He flopped to the floor by our side, apparently inviting himself into our conversation.

"Yeah, but Bourbon wasn't communicating very well back then was he?"

Knight smirked, pulling out a joint and pressing it to his lips.

"Knight!" Rose gasped. "You can't smoke that in here!"

He eyed her lazily, pulling out his lighter but, at the serious look she gave him, he sighed, and stood up.

She pointed towards the back door where I'd entered. "Not even in the building. I don't want you ruining the other dresses."

He shrugged, but began to walk off. "Fine, but if anything happens to you while I'm smoking, Bourbon will take my nuts."

"I'll take your nuts if anything happens," Dante growled from the doorway.

Unlike Knight, he was staying out of ear shot, having the sense to give us our privacy.

Rose waited until Knight had disappeared and Dante was facing away from us to speak. "You're going to be at the wedding right?"

"I think so, but I'm not sure. They haven't told me anything."

"Of course not," she grunted, shaking her head in disappointment. "Heaven forbid men learn how to communicate. I've told Nero that I'm not showing up to the wedding if you can't be there--"

I leaned back, clutching her arms to whisper fiercely, "Rose, if they're forcing you to do this, I swear, I'll find a way to get you out of this. I will burn down the whole chapel if I have to."

She burst out laughing. "I would like to see that. Father Norris would probably call it an act of God."

"I'll do it," I promised fiercely.

She shook her head. "I actually want to marry him."

I narrowed my eyes skeptically. "Are you sure? You don't have to lie to me, Rose."

"No," her eyes were clear, "I swear to you, Aster. I *love* him. I really do." There was a happiness to her gaze that I'd never seen before.

Rose had always been amazing, but every time I'd ever seen her, she'd had this sadness about her. I assumed it was her asshole adoptive father.

But now, she had a calm assurance about her. A brightness. Honestly, she was radiant.

It was like she was glowing.

I inhaled a sharp breath. "Are you pregnant, Rose?"

Her eyes widened. "How did you know?"

I shook my head. "I didn't, except you..." I raised a shoulder, "I don't know, you just look like it. You really look like you're a glowing bubble."

"Well," she bit down on her lower lip, "despite everything that's happened, I really am happy. I really do love Bourbon, and we're going to start a family together." Her cheeks were burning with a soft pinkish tone and her eyes were gleaming. She really was truly luminous.

She wasn't lying.

"But don't tell Coulter, or anyone," she glanced at Dante,

who was still studiously ignoring us, "we haven't told anyone yet."

I made an 'x' over my heart with my finger, nodding. "I swear I won't tell."

She smiled, staring at me, and I couldn't help but smile back.

Her happiness was catching.

Then her smile softened. "Are you okay?"

I pulled in a deep breath. "I'm fine. Considering."

"How is Coulter treating you?"

"Well, he's an ass but what can I say?"

She rolled her eyes. "Of course he's an ass, but he's not hurting you, right?"

"Do you think he would?"

She shook her head, thinking. "No. I would say never, except..." she shook her head, thinking, "except he's different now. Than before." She shook her head again, brushing off the thought. "Look, that doesn't matter, I have something to tell you."

She hesitated, glancing at the door. Then she leaned in, once again whispering against my ear. "Bourbon and I have arranged a way for you to escape from the wedding reception."

I pulled back, my eyes wide, and whisper yelled, "What?"

She nodded. "But you can't tell *anyone*. Not Coulter, not Knight, no one."

"They don't know?"

She shook her head. "No one, except me, Bourbon, and a guy named Torian. During the reception, Torian's going to sneak you out."

"I'm not leaving you, Rose. Why can't you come with me?"

She laughed darkly. "Nero's eyes won't leave me for a minute. Plus, it's too public. But," she put her hand on my arm and squeezed it softly, "don't worry about me. I'm happy, I promise."

I met her eyes, knowing that she was speaking the truth. "Are you sure?"

She nodded, confident. "Yes. Really, Aster. I'm happy. And when this is all over, I'm going to come see you. I promise."

I inhaled a deep breath. "You swear it?"

"Of course," her face turned serious, "but you have to swear to me that you won't tell a soul."

"Not even Coulter?"

"Not even him. It won't work if he knows, it has to be a surprise."

Guilt strummed through me. I was willing to admit, only to myself, of course, that I was beginning to have an itsy, teensy, *trickling*, of feelings for him. Not enough, though, to not want to escape.

But, if things were different, if our worlds were different, things might could work between us.

I had to shut down those feelings.

There was no changing where Coulter came from, no fixing the differences between us.

And yet, still, for some dumb reason, I felt guilty for promising to keep this secret from him.

It was ridiculous. They were keeping me prisoner, for hells sake, but still.

"Aster, you have to swear to me." Rose's eyes were so solemn, so serious, as she stared at me. "You can't tell."

I nodded, inhaling a deep breath. "I swear it."

TWENTY

Coulter

ASTER SHOULD'VE KNOWN BETTER.

My *brother* should've known better.

I'm. Always. Fucking. Watching.

Call me selfish, but I'd worked so hard to get everything set up to sneak Aster out at the same time that Rose would be doing her final fitting, the only time she would be alone enough without my father's watchful eyes.

I just wanted to see the happiness on their faces when, finally, after years of being apart, they were reunited.

And it had been worth it.

Christ, I'd almost teared up myself at the sight of them together like that.

And then, my world came crashing down.

They made arrangements for Aster's escape and didn't trust me enough to tell me.

I wasn't sure who I was more pissed at.

Knight, for not knowing, when he was supposed to be my eyes and ears on Rose.

Bourbon and Rose, for not trusting me that I could help them pull it off.

Or Aster, who'd I'd truly come to feel something for, something I knew was the truth, now that I felt the depth of her betrayal.

It was like the night Lily died all over again, and in one full swoop, I lost everything.

I'd just finished making arrangements with Massimo. Not only did he give me information on Nicholi's weaknesses but he was also coming in with a full team at the wedding, disguised as guests. Furthermore, he'd agreed to meet my father under the pretense of discussing business.

Everything was going exactly to plan when this bombshell dropped, and I felt the ground fall out from under me.

For a whole day, I seethed.

I'd made last minute adjustments and set Aster up as the maid of honor so that she could stand next to Rose at the wedding. I used this as an excuse not to see her, keeping her busy by sending in a team to get her ready for the wedding. She spent the whole day selecting a dress to wear, along with getting waxed, her make up and hair done, everything she would need to be ready for tomorrow.

And yet, all this was a distraction because, the fact was—I couldn't even look at her.

I'd been betrayed. There was no coming back from that.

Ideas came and went with what to do about it.

For hours, I debated about whether or not to let Aster go. To simply do nothing and walk away from her, just like she was walking away from me.

But I had information they didn't have, something I was planning on sharing with Bourbon as soon as I'd set everything up with Massimo.

But that one video changed everything.

Even though I hadn't seen the DNA results from the doctor, I knew that Bourbon wasn't Nero's son.

My father and Bourbon had the same eyes, something that had always bothered Bourbon since he hated our father. But, Uncle Daimon also had the same startling shade of blue, like looking into a turbulent ocean.

Now that Nero knew the truth, Bourbon was as good as dead. What little trust my father had in Bourbon was now demolished.

Nero had invited the whole mafia world to this wedding, announcing that the lost Russian mafia princess had been discovered, and that she was marrying into the Las Vegas outfit. He was also making a big deal about providing the cake, going to great lengths to plan the presentation of it in the middle of the reception.

I didn't trust it.

Nero was at the pinnacle of his career, his 'son' marrying the legendary missing princess of the great Igor Petrov, thought to be dead. Killing them at the wedding made a bold statement, and was exactly something a crazy man like my father would do.

And, as angry as I was at their betrayal, I couldn't let that happen.

No, I needed to follow through with my own plans.

For once, I'd outsmarted my father, and I was going to relish in it tonight.

TWENTY-ONE

Aster

NERO WAS THE ONE TO COLLECT ME.

I was almost flattered.

Out of all the things he needed to do today, he came to threaten *little old me* into behaving.

Fucker.

And where the hell was Coulter? He'd returned late last night, and barely spoke to me before he left again.

Something had changed between us and I didn't know what it was. I'd been giddy after preparing for Rose's wedding but he'd tampered down my excitement quickly by his sour mood.

After gathering some things, claiming he had things he needed to do before the wedding, he'd headed for the door, leaving a cold chill in his wake. He'd stopped when he walked through it, turning to me. "You would never betray me, would you, Aster?"

Any words I had died in my throat, and I could only stare him down with my lips parted, unable to speak.

He waited for what felt like a really long moment, his dark

stare drilling into me. When I didn't say anything, he'd left, and didn't return for the night.

Now, as I stared in the mirror, watched by some beefy baldie named James, one of Nero's guards who looked like the whole world had pissed him off, I decided, *screw it.*

Today, my older sister was getting married to a man she loved.

And, she was going to have a baby.

It was going to be an amazing day and, despite my circumstances, I was determined to enjoy it.

I was ushered to the wedding by Mr. Baldie-face just in time to line up to walk down the aisle.

Rose was stunning in a Claire Pettibone mermaid dress, with a gorgeous lace bodice and delicate hand-stitched beading. Her chestnut-brown hair cascaded down her back in soft waves, with strands of it threaded through delicately placed aster, lily, and rose flowers.

I teared up at the sight of her homage to me and my sister.

Her face lit up the moment she saw me, and we hugged enthusiastically before a pale, long faced woman urged us to our places.

I walked somberly down the row towards the altar, resisting the urge to skip. I recognized Bourbon from the photo Rose had shown me, staring up the aisle. His stark, blue eyes looked eager and totally smitten, and a warmth washed through me.

Life was going to be good for her.

Despite the threat of Nero, he would protect and take care of her.

Coulter was standing next to him, and I tried to catch his eyes, but he didn't look at me. A few men down from them stood another man, with almond shaped eyes, long hair tied behind him, and danger radiating from his mere essence.

He also had a chocolate cosmos flower pinned to his suit,

the only man wearing such a flower. This was my sign: he was the man who would help me escape. His eyes met mine in a meaningful stare and I nodded briefly, rushing to my spot.

My smile wavering, I took my place and waited patiently, torn between being so happy and excited for Rose, feeling sad about Coulter's change in behavior, and nervous about my plans for escape.

My stomach rolled every time I thought about it, guilt plaguing me.

I wanted to tell Coulter, I really did. But in the short time I'd had to say something last night, I'd opened my mouth, intending to tell him, but nothing came out. Rose said *no one*, and I had to keep my promise.

The wedding was beautiful, although Rose didn't have much time to talk to me, so I mingled, meeting men and women from all over the world. There seemed to be a common, underlying feel to the audience.

Most of the people here were mafia.

In the end, I ended up hanging out with a scowling Dante for the rest of the day and through the beginning of the reception. Just as everyone was sitting for the wedding dinner, I glanced towards the table at the head of the room.

Coulter was standing behind it, talking to his father. They were next to Bourbon, who was pulling out a chair for Rose.

I fidgeted, not knowing where to go, when Coulter looked my way.

His golden eyes met mine for the first time today. Suddenly the world around me fell away and it was just me and him.

I knew in my heart that I couldn't betray him.

Despite the fact that he was helping keep me prisoner, he could've been so much worse.

Could've treated me how Nero treated those women.

Despite everything, Coulter had not only been good to me,

but he'd wiggled his way into my heart, and I knew that I couldn't leave him.

Not like this.

And possibly, not eve—I stopped the thought in its tracks.

He looked away, giving a significant look to Dante, and I pulled in a deep breath.

I had to talk to Rose, tell her I wasn't leaving. I felt like I was letting her down, but if I could just explain to her how I felt about Coulter, how kind he'd been to me, she would understand.

Trying to be discreet, since I was leaving just as everyone was sitting down to eat, I ducked low, making my way towards the side of the room. I'd hoped to be discreet by avoiding the crowd in the middle of the room.

As soon as I made it to the wall, a hand clasped around my arm.

It was Dante. His cold eyes stared at me with disdain, and I faltered, trying to swallow down the lump in my now, suddenly dry throat.

He looked at me as if I was a bedbug on his pillow.

Did he know about the plans to escape?

The blood drained from my face. Why else would he look at me like that?

It wasn't possible. *It couldn't be.*

I tried to pull my arm away but his fingers tightened, stepping into me to growl in my ear. "Coulter has requested your presence by his side for the meal."

I tried to pull away again but his arm was a steel bar around me. I'd have to make a scene to get away.

"Sure," I gave him a false smile, trying not to show my nervousness. "I just need to talk to my sister first."

If possible, his eyes grew colder. "Oh, I don't think that's going to happen."

If I was reading the signs right, Coulter knew about the escape.

I don't know how he knew, but somehow he'd found out, and he thought I was betraying him.

Well, I'd just have to explain myself to him, wouldn't I?

"Let me go," I growled, "and I will follow you willingly to the front."

He stared into my face, assessing me. Then, after a moment, he leaned in. "Do you remember my promise to you?"

I straightened, meeting his gaze with a defiant one of my own. "Yes. Do you remember my promise *to you?*"

His fingers dug even more harshly into my skin, though he did put some distance between my knee and his nuts. "I don't trust people who betray Coulter, so no, I'm not letting you go. You will walk with me to the front, and you will do as Coulter asks."

I stiffened but decided that, for Rose's sake, I wasn't going to make a scene.

I *let* Dante lead me to the front of the room, and as soon as we passed the front table, all eyes moved to me.

For the first time in a long time, I felt self-conscious as hundreds of faces stared at me, watching as Dante escorted me across the back table to Coulter.

When we arrived, Coulter didn't look at me and I shifted nervously. Next to Coulter, sat the empty chair where Dante had been assigned to sit, then Knight.

After that were people I didn't recognize.

I looked up at Rose, trying to capture her attention, but she was already staring at me, a smile frozen on her face. Her mouth moved, but I couldn't understand what she was trying to say. The waiters began to serve the appetizers.

"Sit down, Aster," Coulter growled. Since I didn't see any other empty seat, I edged towards Dante's empty chair, but

Coulter's hand snapped out, grabbing my arm and dragging me to him, where he unceremoniously dumped me into his lap.

I landed with a yelp, clasping my hand over my mouth to muffle the embarrassing noise.

Dios mio, how humiliating. Was Coulter expecting me to eat on his lap the whole time? I was never going to be able to talk to Rose now.

I shifted, and Coulter leaned forward, his hand tight on my waist to hold me still, and growled in my ear. "You nervous, Aster?"

I faked a smile, though I was super uneasy. "I don't know how you expect me to eat like this."

"It's easy, let me show you," he picked up a spoon and, leaning into my back, the warmth of his firm chest bleeding into me, filled it with soup, then pressed it to my lips.

"Really," I tried to talk him down from this madness, "this isn't necessary."

"It really is." His mouth closed over the lobe of my ear, nibbling it, "Smile, Aster, people are staring."

The attention was still on us, stern faces gazing. Probably wondering who the 'whore' was on his lap. Some almost looked offended, like I was making a spectacle on purpose, even though they'd just seen me practically dragged up here. Some of the men stared with sly smirks, a few women however, gave me a sympathetic smile.

I straightened, meeting their gazes, and opened my mouth.

Spiced tomato-based flavors exploded on my tongue, and I murmured as it slid down my throat.

Bit by bit, his hand went from his plate to my mouth, his fingers brushing sensually over my lips, with one hand clamped around my stomach, his body pressed tight against my back.

The wine was like silk, the salmon rich, and the soft lights around us shimmering.

I fell into a trance, with the wine and his warmth surrounding me, the smell of his musk tickling my senses, his lips pressing to my ear.

I was vaguely aware of his thickening cock at my back, Knight talking and laughing with Coulter, and Nero growing more and more drunk.

My skin buzzed each time Coulter's fingers made contact with my lips, while his other hand was slowly drawing up my dress, pulling it up and over my knee.

Then his fingers began to softly stroke the skin of my inner thigh, setting my heart racing.

It was warm, stifling almost.

Suddenly, I was aware of everything in the room.

How close Nero was to the two of us, shifting agitatedly. Did he know what Coulter was doing?

Strangely, Rose and Bourbon were missing from the table, their two seats empty like missing diamonds in a ring setting.

Had Rose tried to get my attention?

My cheeks burned an even deeper shade of red at the thought. I'd been so mesmerized by the opulent food and Coulter's touch, I hadn't noticed them leave.

Coulter's hand trickled higher under my dress, his fingers tickling across the lace of my softness.

"Open your legs, Aster," he murmured against my ear, and I obeyed, unable to stop myself.

And, even though he went back to talking to some guy named Massimo and Nero, who was growing more and more agitated, even though I could see Torian with his signature flower trying to capture my gaze meaningfully, I held my breath, not moving, as Coulter's finger slipped under the line of my panties. Parting my pussy lips, he began to stroke me.

Oh. God.

Fire blazed through me. I was already wet.

I wanted him to stop. God, did I want him to keep going.

I was amazed no one even glanced at his hand, mostly hidden by the tablecloth, but if anyone really wanted to, they would be able to see.

I was vaguely aware of the commotion at the end of the room, the whispers that began in a trickle and slowly swelled through the room.

Then, as Coulter inserted two fingers up inside me, pumping up into me, my bald, beefy guard walked up to Nero to whisper in his ear, placing something in his hand.

"Well then, find them," Nero snarled, banging his hand on the table.

I vaguely registered that he'd slammed down a syringe needle, and that the cake was being brought from the back of the room through the crowd. That the mood of the room was shifting from curiosity to alarm.

Were Rose and Bourbon missing?

What was going on?

I tried to care, I really did.

And just as I opened my mouth to ask, Coulter inserted another finger up inside me, pressing against my clit with his thumb.

Oh my god, I was going to come, right in front of everyone.

I clutched the table, my insides screaming, my whole body flaming with need.

And yet, I needed to find Rose.

I moved to stand, knowing Coulter would have to pull out if I did, but his other hand came down on my hip, squeezing it. His voice was a growling demand. "Stay."

I stilled, surprised by the commanding sneer in his tone. He leaned forward, shoving a third finger up inside me roughly as he bit out in my ear. "You're not thinking of leaving, are you Aster?"

My lips parted as he fucked me relentlessly, trying to speak. "I—I wasn't, I mean, I was going to tell you--"

"You were going to run, Aster." I could hear the hurt in his voice, the low growl that betrayed his pain, "You betrayed me. For that, you need to be punished. You're *not* leaving. Not if you want to save your sister."

My breath left me in an exhale. I was speechless.

Coulter continued to fuck me with his fingers and I could only clench around him, biting down on my lip to keep myself from moaning.

Then, the baker made it to the front of the room, carting the large cake in front of him. It was white, with a strawberry sauce, dripping from all sides.

I vaguely registered his eyes wide in fear as he stared, not at where he was walking, but at the cake.

Nero jerked to his feet with a growl, grabbing the microphone at the table.

"Ladies and gentlemen..." I realized with a shock that it wasn't Nero speaking, but Coulter.

All eyes were suddenly on him, *and me.*

He didn't let up on my cunt, but increased his thrusting. It was all I could do to clutch the table tight and not show everyone that I was about to come all over Coulter's fingers.

"I know I'm terrible, stealing the spotlight like this on the bride and groom's day, but I can't hold it back any longer."

I stared blankly at the cake that was now featured in the front of the room, realizing with horror that what I thought was the cake topper was actually two eyeballs.

Actual. Real. Eyeballs.

They were a deep blue, and reminded me of a stormy sea. Eyes that also reminded me of Bourbon's.

What I thought was strawberry sauce was actually *blood*, dripping from the top, all the way down the sides.

What the fuck was going on?

"As you know," Coulter continued, "Rose Petrov, now King, is the lost Russian princess. She's graced us with her beauty and bloodline, and it truly is our honor to have her in our family." He paused dramatically, flicking my clit with his thumb, and I wanted to *kill* him, "but what you might not know is that we've also discovered her sister, Aster." All eyes were suddenly on me, and Nero growled from beside us. "What the hell are you doing, Coulter?"

Coulter looked up at his father, a mocking grin on his face as he crooned. "I'm telling you we're in love, father. Aster has agreed to be my wife. Haven't you, baby?" He hooked his fingers up inside me, tap tap tapping once again on that magical spot up inside me.

I couldn't help it.

No matter how much I pressed my thighs together, how much I grit my teeth, I couldn't stop it.

I stared at those two blue eyes, and came.

And fucking came.

I creamed all over his fingers and hand, and my panties and thighs were soaked, all while everyone was staring at me.

Then, chuckling darkly, he pressed his lips to my ear, kissing it and whispering, "I'll lick that up later, little nightmare."

To be continued...

DOWNLOAD THE NEXT BOOK HERE.

Also, join my text list for a FREE prequel.

ABOUT THE AUTHOR

Ivy Mason is obsessed with enigmatic men who observe from the darkness, speak with their eyes, and dominate with the smoky command of their voice.

✮ She's the #1 best selling author in her neighborhood (she guesses),

✮ was a five-time winner of the best burper prize in her household -- until she lost the title to her daughter, who holds the all time championship for two years running,

✮ and is the recipient of the 'worst-speller award' from her editor.

She likes her hair colorful, her music loud, lots of italics in her writing, and is addicted to the word fuck.

Find out more about her on her website at ivymason.org.